Also by Goran Simić

Immigrant Blues
Brick Books, 2003

From Sarajevo, With Sorrow
Biblioasis, 2005

YESTERDAY'S PEOPLE

GORAN SIMIĆ

YESTERDAY'S PEOPLE

STORIES

BIBLIOASIS

FIRST EDITION

Library and Archives Canada Cataloguing in Publication

Simić, Goran, 1952-
Yesterday's people / Goran Simić.

0-9735971-8-6 (LIMITED ED, CASED)
0-9735971-7-8 (PBK)

1. Sarajevo (Bosnia and Herzegovina)—History—Siege,
1992-1996-Fiction. 2. Emigration and immigration—
Fiction. 3. War stories, Canadian (English). I. Title.

PS8587.I3119Y48 2005   C813'.54   C2005-905290-2

edited by
DANIEL WELLS

PRINTED AND BOUND IN CANADA

CONTENTS

NINA

I MET NINA YESTERDAY. I WISH I HADN'T.

She was walking across a massive steel beam—the only remainder of a pretty wooden bridge that resisted fire for two days, and then burned down. With two canisters of water in her hands, she balanced on that beam. At the other end I waited, in a long line of clamouring people waiting for water reeking of chlorine. There was no time to move away.

I had had a terrible night and I was not ready to talk. Somebody working with us in the city morgue had stolen some gold jewelry from the corpses pulled out of the river that night. It might have been ignored had the boys from the Military Police not come just before midnight to take away the body of some young sergeant and noticed that a pistol was missing from his holster. They threatened to shoot us all. Maybe they would have, had they not gone to the morgue director and found the pistol in his hand. He shot himself in the basement of his house. He shot his wife first. We were told to go home, but nobody wanted to, fearing gossip about the stolen gold. We all felt safer in the morgue than we did in our homes.

We were all slowly going mad.

A shadow of what used to be Nina Rosh moved towards me. Once a girl to whose beauty no one was immune, Nina filled the boring concerts of the Sarajevo Philharmonic Orchestra with aroused high school boys rather than enthusiasts

9

of Mozart. Her middle-aged violoncello professor suddenly divorced his wife, and after a brief bout of drinking, disappeared from this city of gossip and exaggeration.

This same Nina looks at me from an old photograph, from a time when we wore our love and youth like a banner.

I barely recognized her.

We met last a few days before war entered the city through cannon barrels, bumping into one another at the graveyard gates. Her young cousin, with whom she walked arm-in-arm, could not hide his embarrassment. I couldn't either. Only a few locks remained of her long blonde hair sticking out from a woolen cap, and a red disfigurement, like paint spilled by an artist, ran from her left ear to the corner of her lips. Words poured out of her, though I could not understand their sense. Then her cousin dragged her away and she poured that chaos of words on him alone. On that occasion she turned only the right side of her face toward me.

❖ ❖ ❖

She no longer paid any attention to such vanity. She embraced me, a ruined house leaning against a neighbouring building, tiredly, as if struggling not to fall down.

A shell whistled above our heads and we scrambled for the first gateway, instinctively, without surprise and before fear. Sorrow sets in later, when we hear the news and the names of those who heard that sound for the last time. The number of those grows daily.

We sat down on a stairway. An ant walked across the lapel of her coat.

"I started to smoke at the worst time. I can't stop any

more." She did not try to hide the trembling hand that held the burning match. Nobody hides that any more. We all have trembling hands.

"Imagine," she went on, "I got only half a kilo of tobacco for my mother's wedding ring the other day. Those thieves. If I was in the government I would lock them all up. Maybe that's why I drink. I drink when I have it. I used to get pure alcohol from the hospital when I worked there, but I couldn't stand the blood. Dad says artists and blood do not go together. They told me I should be ashamed, that the wounded need it more. But they drank it too. They poured it in their tea, or sold it. I'm not stupid."

Sirens sounded an alarm. They're always too late. Nobody pays attention to them any more. I watched two kids sitting in a garbage bin, picking through tin cans, searching for scraps of food. Who knows where they came from. The city is full of refugees waiting patiently for hours in line-ups at the humanitarian kitchens, while packs of children freely roam. Some children lie in the morgue for days without anyone claiming the bodies. We bury them in common graves.

"I heard that you have a child, too," Nina said, taking a break, barely long enough to catch her breath.

"I do." She could hardly have been more interested had I said no.

At the beginning of the war my wife and son took refuge in Italy. I stayed behind, believing the fighting to be a mere misunderstanding. I received only a single letter, a long time ago, and then lost track of them. But yesterday a foreign reporter brought me a letter. It would have been better if he hadn't. She was seeking a divorce. She wanted to live in Canada, with some Italian. Our marriage hadn't been much, but

I'd expected something more than mere formality. She advised selling the apartment, if it was not already destroyed. My son added a few lines as well. I understood none of them. They were in Italian.

❖ ❖ ❖

Through someone's apartment door could be heard the day's news. I missed the names of the wounded. I will catch up with the dead tonight anyway. The broadcast ended with the anthem of the city's defenders and a recommendation not to move around the city unless absolutely necessary. We walk around dead.

"It is nice to have someone," said Nina. "My dad is all I have left. He had a stroke last year, half his body is paralyzed. He's confined to a bed. Did you know that?"

"No." Even if I had, I doubt I'd have felt much compassion. Twenty years ago the thought might even have gladdened me. Now I don't care. It doesn't even hurt to remember him the way he was in those days.

"Young man," he'd addressed me the first time we met in front of his door, "the next time it comes into your mind to visit us, and I pray that it will not, I expect that you will pay a visit to the barber first, and put on something befitting this decent home."

He enjoyed my discomfort too much to notice the sadness on Nina's face. I meant to tell him that Nina and I had loved each other for a long time, so he'd better get used to it. But I did not.

Now, I realize that he did not hate only me. He hated the way my generation negated his own, revolting against their blind dedication to principles born after a war long past. He cashed in on his patriotism over and over again. Once a poor rural shepherd, now a wealthy former partisan, he struggled not to have that shepherd in himself recognized once more. So, while we fought over Nina, she just kept crying. In the balance, between obedience and love, Nina discovered sorrow.

Her father and I may have even enjoyed that emotional tug of war. Nina did not. He would burst into our high school during our breaks just to prevent me from seeing her for a brief while, but I knew the porter of the theatre, and he secretly let me into her dressing room. Her father managed to discover the very last ally who helped me arrange our secret meetings, his own wife, who subsequently wore a black eye for a while. But I knew their mailman, who often showed up at their door at precisely the moment her father stepped out. He brought me news that Nina's professor of violoncello kept hanging around the house longer and longer, and that her father regularly left at that time.

That old garbage used all the means at his disposal to keep me away from Nina. I dreamt up ways of endearing myself to him, but it always ended up in a fantasy about his sudden demise. Letters and brief encounters were an insufficient compensation for the brush fire I carried within me.

❖ ❖ ❖

Curses floated across the river. There was no water again. People began dispersing like a disgraced army, dragging their empty canisters. Some kept waiting. Others put their canisters underneath the eaves to collect rain.

A shell whistled past again. Mothers called to children, checking to see whether they were in the shelter. Nina stopped talking for an instant, just long enough to light a new cigarette. Her fingers played with a thread on her coat, a lingering memory of a button. An ant crawled across her neck. She did not feel it. Two weeks ago, when I decided to stop smoking, I left one cigarette in my pocket. I felt it there at that moment. Two weeks, here, are like a lifetime.

"I watched you once on television," she said, winding the little thread around her finger. "I mean, when we still had electricity. I did not understand a single word you said. It was as if you were trying to make a house of words to hide in."

"You have such a house, too. Your violoncello."

"That is not my house. It is just an instrument." She stared at my face, surprised that I did not understand her the way that I should. Then, she examined the left half of my face, the one I always instinctively try to hide from people I'm talking to.

"I did not know that you had such a big scar."

"One could make a decent face out of our two halves." But she didn't seem to hear me.

"You know, when I was in the hospital, there was a guy who wanted to cut my hair and another who kept scratching my face." She spoke without a break, fixated on my scar.

I reached into my pocket for the cigarette and lit it, just to hide from her gaze. My scar, running across my cheek and chin, started to sting. I knew that I must be imagining it. Scars don't sting. They ache.

❖ ❖ ❖

14

Nina first went to the madhouse directly after a concert, at a time when jealousy nibbled away at me due to the gossip surrounding the sudden divorce of her professor. That was a painful time. I used to spend my days by the telephone expecting her call, but she called ever less frequently. Postcards from her tours was all that there was.

I was at that concert. The conductor repeated the beginning after Nina started playing some popular tune. The audience rewarded her mischief with a long applause, the first time. The next time nobody laughed any more. Nina rested her violoncello on the chair, stood up and started to sing some crude little ditties, swearing.

The silence was nauseating. Her father jumped out of his front row seat and carried her off the stage. I could hear her begging to finish her song. I ran to her dressing room. The porter did not block my way.

Through her half open door I heard slaps, her father screaming.

"Pull yourself together! Pull yourself together! You must not do this to me. You must not!" He shouted into the pained grimace that remained of Nina's face. She was already drifting away.

It was then that he saw me standing in the doorway. Hatred, sharp as a slap, flashed across his face. He reached into his jacket, likely for his non-existent pistol, then kicked the door with so much force that I flew through the door of the dressing room across the corridor and crashed on top of a pile of music stands. The last I heard was someone shrieking.

When I woke, a doctor hovering above me explained that I had devilish luck. Half my face wrapped in bandages, they took me home. I had a headache for days. I sat in a room by the telephone under the watchful eye of my mother, who left only occasionally to see the lawyer and plan the charges.

In the end she gave up. She would go briefly to church and return with the smell of frankincense about her. It was all the same to me. I heard her tell her favourite proverb to someone on the phone. Only three things in life could not be hidden: a cough, poverty and love.

❖ ❖ ❖

A thick rain began to fall. I love rain, because then they stop shelling the city. Two soldiers passed down the street dragging a tree trunk with a rope. One of them said something to the two prostitutes who waved from a deserted shop. The city is full of prostitutes and the army is getting poorer.

Nina did not stop talking. She stared at a wall, lining up sentences that rang through the empty stairwell. An ant crawled underneath her ear. She did not notice it.

"We rented a room to some soldier but he was a boor. He became so brazen that he once pushed me to play the anthem for him and my dad said that playing the anthem is the lowest abasement for a musician. He deserved to become a casualty at the front. Dad would have thrown him out of the apartment, but then it happened . . ."

"Let's go," I said. "They've stopped shooting."

"How can I smoke, then? You're lucky that you don't smoke."

"I will take your canisters. Mine are empty anyway."

"You are really kind."

"For old time's sake."

"But how will I smoke in the rain?"

A soldier came down the stairs. He cursed the war, the rain and the enemy. He did not recognize me. A couple of months ago he came to the morgue. He identified his sister's body by the ring on her finger. He refused to take anything she owned, but then came back in the evening, drunk, with a gun, wanting to shoot me. We barely restrained him. I had simply asked him to sign a form before he took her ring.

❖ ❖ ❖

It took two months to find out where Nina was. Her mother finally told me. Her madness was rarely mentioned, and then only as an aside, while the rage of the city fell upon the professor of violoncello, drowning in his alcohol. Nobody ever mentioned me.

They placed Nina in a mountain hospital, far from the city, a primitive madhouse enclosed within a tall fence. They wouldn't let me see her. My name was on the list of the unwanted and the receptionist quite roughly told me that it would be best if I caught the first bus back to where I'd come from. Of course, I did not.

I circled the hospital and saw her in a courtyard behind a tall wire fence, walking, muttering some children's song. Even in those stained hospital pajamas she was beautiful. But when I called her she did not recognize me. I told her that I came to take her away, that I'd arranged with a relative in Belgrade to take us in. But she said she couldn't leave, because she had to practice a song for the hospital performance.

I kept showing her our photograph, reminding her of our oath that we would never part, but Nina was far away. She looked at me as if through a mist, trying to figure out why I did not want her to take part in the hospital performance. I couldn't stand the fact that Nina was crazy, and that I belonged to the world of shadows. She started to scream when I tried to jump the fence. The guards came and I ended my journey with a few slaps across my face and a ride in a police car, back to the city. The policeman who took me home told me before he left that I wasn't the only one who could not accept things the way they were, and that I was the easiest case of the day.

"I have become a taxi driver," he told me as I stood there crying, delivered into the hands of my mother.

❖ ❖ ❖

Nina walked beside me, trying to relight her damp cigarette. She wouldn't stop talking about her father, who did not understand how hard it is to get medicine. She said that she even phoned her old hospital, but that it was now an army barracks. She spoke of her hospital with sorrow, as if about her homeland.

An ant crawled under her lip. I reached out to remove it.

"Don't hurt me, please!" she screamed and ran. I have not seen such horror in any face before, and I see horror daily at the morgue. What did she see in the movement of my hand, reaching out for an ant that behaved as if there was no difference between Nina and a wall?

For a moment, I thought that she'd woken up from a long deep dream, bringing back the choking question I had been carrying around for years like an empty wallet. Had she recognized me at that moment? I don't know.

It seemed to me that in her wide open eyes I saw the same

Nina I'd last seen in an old photograph. I dashed after her, but Nina kept running away. I watched her running down the street, drenched in rain, a crumbling cigarette in her mouth. My two empty canisters in her hands.

I wanted to ask her about the man recently brought into the morgue during an exchange of the dead. He had little to identify him, except for a tattoo on his left arm, at the height of his heart. It read Nina Rosh. We buried him under that name. I put that name in the book of the dead in an even handwriting that never betrayed the curiosity I felt. It is like the sting of a scar.

❖ ❖ ❖

I see people off everyday. We who remain walk around the city like shadows, and we all fantasize a bit that we will wake up one day at the place where our nightmare had begun. One day I will put the name of Nina's father among those of the other passers-by, and that will remove the last proof that I was the young man smiling in that photograph. The ant from Nina's face will then disappear as well.

I wonder if a day might come when I will not even believe that I met Nina. I wish I had not.

MINEFIELD

AT THE BEGINNING of the war they called us "Wolves," and we were terribly proud of that—no less proud than we were later enraged when someone from city headquarters nick-named us "Pensioners." There were ten of us protecting a fifty metre wide ravine up on top of Black Hill and we were doing it perfectly well, especially considering that we were holding real weapons for the first time in our lives. We were all volunteers, and many had picked up a gun more out of curiosity than from any real feeling that we needed to defend the city from the crazed, armed peasants who were getting ready for this war long before we'd even given it a thought.

It all seemed out of a movie until the day the student we called Rambo tried to use a bow and arrow to launch a hand grenade. We spent days scraping bits and pieces of his head off of the bunker wall and the nearby trees. It might sound stupid, but we were almost thankful that he died—it forced the rest of us to grow up quickly. Afterwards, we left the movies to the actors and focussed on the weight of the rifle in our hands and the heat of the helmet on our heads. Buried in muddy trenches deep in the bush, we were like house plants stuck in the desert.

In the beginning, we jumped every time an owl hooted. Later, we paid little attention to the howling of the hungry wolves in the mountains. The only things that reminded us of the city were the empty face-cream boxes we used to store our booze money.

The enemy only tried to break through our line once. We thrashed them so badly that they left behind two dead soldiers, some weapons and an overturned armoured personnel carrier. Those two dead boys, whose pockets contained nothing but some unused postage stamps and a couple of porn magazines, were credited to me, and I did not deny it, even though I was quite sure I'd never fired in their direction.

We traded those two dead bodies for a live cow. We put the corpses on a sled and they pulled it across; at the same time we dragged over to our side the skinny and terrified cow. The cow died before dawn because the bastards had poisoned it, and she was later counted as one of the last casualties in the defence of Black Hill. We were bothered by being duped much more than we were about having to drag the dead cow far from our trenches to bury it.

The next morning we attacked them out of sheer revenge, though we only succeeded in using up most of our remaining ammunition and in siphoning about fifty litres of diesel oil from their overturned carrier.

Later, we made another deal with them, a carton of their cigarettes for a canister of our oil. The cigarettes arrived; then they pulled with a rope the oil canister we had pissed in as much as we could. They cursed our mothers from their trenches, and threatened to shoot our families once they broke into the city. We promised them as much—public hangings in the city square—as soon as we realized that our cigarettes had arrived wet. They'd probably pissed on them.

After that, we stopped trading goods and attacking one another. We listened to the news on our transistor radios, cheering the way we used to at soccer games whenever we heard that the peasants had been defeated on some front or another. The peasants across the battlefield responded simi-larly, shooting at the trees above our heads whenever the for-tunes of war favoured their side. They did it to us more often than we did it to them.

As time passed and our ammunition dwindled, we shot less and swore more. We threw empty bottles of brandy at them, and loudly reminisced about buying their wives and sisters with pairs of nylon stockings. In turn, they lobbed in our direction bare sheep bones and blown up condoms tied to stones with our flag scribbled on them.

Everything was only beginning. We went mad after one of our best, Basketman, a rising star on our local basketball team, stretched his middle finger above the trench, only to lose it to a sniper's bullet. He screamed, and we all scrambled in a panic looking for his finger in the muddy trenches.

The wind blew laughter from the other side. "No more sex with your darling," someone called. "Give us her address when she wants a baby."

After Lamb tried without success to stop the bleeding, I sent Basketman back down to the city. I was wrong to send him alone. A few days later, a courier brought a message from our captain, who called me brainless. On his way back, the outraged Basketman had emptied his machine gun into a field of sheep and cows.

"And what the hell does your Basketman mean about these slings you've made for fun? Would you rather I sent toys next time instead of food and ammunition?" I wrote back that Basketman had probably lost his mind. The great-est lesson I learned during the war was not to admit to mistakes.

Actually, with suspenders stretched between two wooden

poles, we had made a mighty sling, capable of hurling at the enemy anything we didn't need anymore. They soon did the same, and the fear of a barrage of stones soon matched our fear of sniper bullets. Basketman had been our champion. Every time he took aim, we would hear a scream or curse from the peasants. Poor Basketman. I heard that he was rejected by the second league basketball team and ended up going to the Army sniper unit.

The fifty odd metres of space between us soon resembled a garbage dump, and the air reverberated with our escalating taunts. There was so much garbage that we could only barely make out those green metal heads, no bigger than mushrooms planted in the soil. The little green heads of our nightmares, as we planned how to attack the enemy. The little green heads of our strategies, as we thought about the enemy's possible offensive.

"When this war is over, I'm going to send those bastards over there to clean up all that mess with brooms," the guy we called Birdy dreamt. We never learned his real name because he was soon shot by a sniper while trying to climb up a maple tree to reach a wild pigeon's nest.

After I sent Birdy's corpse to HQ, a strange looking soldier from Special Forces arrived with a sniper who stayed one night only, shot two soldiers across the minefield, and left so abruptly that he too remained anonymous.

"Give me a break. Fucking amateur," he said when I asked him for his name to put in my report. He disappeared into the night, laughing about our slings.

After he left, the war seemed to slow.

The bags of shit we threw at one another piled up on the battlefield. By mid-summer it stank so badly that each side

24

agreed to stop. The arsenal of verbal obscenities, however, continued to escalate. As we could not see each other, each side nicknamed the other from what could be guessed by the sound of their voices. The most vocal on their side we called Ass, Cock, Cretin and Guts. They, in turn, christened us Bastard, Vulture, Lamb and Turd. I was called Sickness, probably because of my endless coughing, caused by too much smoking.

As time went on, no one reacted to the cursing of mothers and sisters any more: that was something that only younger, denser soldiers reveled in. Originality became the order of the day, the assaults by which we earned our stripes. We came to know, over time, who on their side was the easiest to provoke, as well as the relative intelligence of each by what they reacted to. They knew just as well who among us had the weakest nerves.

We would cheer up whenever Cock started shouting from their side. A stupid and nervous little peasant, he could never take an insult without blowing up. Once we unnerved him so much that he opened fire on us until Guts screamed that if he did not quit he'd send him off to a real battlefield. It was our Vulture who had ticked him off.

"Little Coooock, listen up, let me tell you something."

"What do you want Vulture? If you are hungry, go to the toilet."

"I am not kidding. I think your mother was right."

"What are you trying to say?"

"Well, the last time I fucked your mother, she told me to put on a condom or I'd make her a cretin. Judging by you, I guess she was right."

After that, all of our taunts took as their object Cock's

mother, and it took us days to realize that he was either forbidden to talk back or had left for some other battlefield.

The weakest link on our side was Turd, a pimpled, stupid soldier who had come to Sarajevo a couple of years before the war. He married a pretty daughter from a prosperous Muslim family and quickly opened a burek shop. After sending his wife to safety in Germany, he evaded military recruitment for six months, hiding in his shop. They found him only after the city's power was cut, and the stink of his rotting meat became unbearable. His neighbours never forgave him for never once thinking of their hunger while sitting surrounded by mounds of soon to be rotting food. The city authorities sent him to me, not knowing what else to do with him. I sent him to the city every three days in order to get provisions, but also because I knew that no one would embellish our victories and heroism more fabulously than he. It was necessary that we feed this kind of tripe to our headquarters.

When not fetching provisions, I would send him to replenish the ammunition reserves we kept wasting in our futile hunting of rabbits and pheasants. Besides, we all preferred that he practice his religious observances at the mosque, as opposed to our cramped bunker, where he interfered with our cards. All of us felt him like scabies.

Furthermore, Turd was pathologically jealous, and would leave our bunker when we started telling idle tales about wives and their lovers, one of our universal themes. He once did not speak a word to any of us for two days when we commented on a photograph of his wife, telling him that she was a *good piece*.

Turd left the impression that God had made him out of leftovers. Worse than this was the fact that in our verbal warfare, when we desperately needed to stick it to the other side, his score was catastrophic. His repertoire went no further than cursing their mothers and families, and even when he managed to figure out something smarter, someone from the opposite camp would silence him so severely that everyone in our trench felt ashamed for him. We could forgive bad jokes for the first three months or so, but half a year of verbal warfare demanded at least some originality; without it, there was no way of escaping humiliation.

On one occasion Turd almost got killed because of his stupidity. He crossed voices with Guts, whose deep resonant voice resounded as if from a cave. Guts was a witty joker whose jabs at our expense burned like shots. In spite of the contempt we felt for him as an enemy, the sound of his voice brought a grudging respect.

That day, we'd heard news on the radio that had killed our last hope that the war would end soon. Turd started howling across the field, out of sheer neurosis, I suppose, that they were murderers and robbers, and that only savages could tear down mosques.

"That is no good. We do not like to touch other people's faith either," came Guts' conciliatory voice.

"Why then do you keep tearing them down?" Turd foamed.

"We have figured out something better. We're producing blow-up mosques, like balloons, so the next time we open fire, you can quickly deflate it and transfer it someplace else, before it gets hit."

Out of his mind, Turd jumped out of the trench, gun in hand. Had we not grabbed his legs and pulled him back in, the machine-gun fire that burst across the leaves above our heads would have cut him down.

❖ ❖ ❖

As autumn approached, we still growled at one another, though we were perfectly happy to have escaped the city below, where we could hear shells exploding. We opened fire a couple of times at the female underwear one of them raised up on a stick, claiming that they were a souvenir from Turd's wife.

Soon after, there was silence for several days. They didn't respond to our provocations, nor could we smell the cooking from their trenches. And then one night they retreated to their reserve positions, leaving us their old trenches, with a minefield between us.

I informed Headquarters about the conquest of fifty odd metres of space. Instead of congratulations, an order arrived to send back all but two of my soldiers. The minefield between us meant that we would now function as little more than sentries. I did not relish being thrown into retirement, in spite of being one of the most experienced fighters, but neither did I ignore the fact that winter was coming and we had plenty of firewood. Nobody waited for me in the city anyways. I put slips of paper labelled "city" and "bush" into a hat and each of us drew to decide who would stay. Turd drew bush, which he immediately took as a sign of bad luck. My other soldier was Lamb, a medical student to whom nothing made any difference any more, ever since he'd buried both his father and mother within a week in the early days of the war.

The others packed up and left, promising that they would regularly comfort our girlfriends. They promised to send us instruction manuals on how to use a shower and blow drier.

We really did stink like skunks. Although I washed my socks and underwear daily, I could still smell their stench as they dried on a rack near the fire, metres away.

Smoke rose up from the other side of the field and everything went on as before, though it was soon apparent that they were also at least halved. The only known voice that remained came from Guts. The others obviously belonged to some pubescent kids who were just mutating. They shouted lies about what they'd had for dinner, dreams of steaks and french fries, but we could smell their burned kidney beans; we made up stories about octopus salad, even though canned meat was the only food we'd tasted in months. I would fire a bullet into the bush from time to time, shouting that I had just killed a deer, but our cauldron kept smelling of kidney beans and disgusting canned food.

That is when it happened.

Cleaning out some garbage the peasants had left behind, Turd discovered a bundle of documents and started reading. They were applications for divorce that lawyers from foreign countries were sending by courier to our besieged city. I knew the whole story: after the first year of war it was whispered all around, a public secret. Two soldiers blew their heads off and ten more tried to escape from the city barracks to reach the countries from which the divorce applications were coming. The military authorities wrote the documents off as enemy war propaganda, as psychological warfare intended to weaken our morale. I had no one waiting for me, in Sarajevo or elsewhere, so I paid the furor scant attention; I used the Headquarters' release on the subject to roll my tobacco. Turd knew too much about this for me to feed him any lies about the special war—only children would have

29

believed such tales anyways. He was furious when I gathered up all of the documents to send them to Headquarters.

"Look at this whore," he screamed, trembling, showing me a piece of paper. "Her husband lost both legs putting out a fire in their house, so she would have a place to come back to with their child—and now she wants to divorce him . . ."

"Don't scream," I said. "Those fools across will hear you . . ."

"How can I stop screaming? Screw their harlot mothers! We are dying here so that they will have a place to come back to, while they warm beds for their Germans and Italians!"

He was screaming so loudly that I grabbed him by the neck to try and shut him up. He tore the insignia off of my shirt. I could have cared less: I was half decommissioned anyway. The next day he apologized. He spent the next two days using a tin can to throw mud out of our trench. He made a roof out of leaves. He talked to no one.

I did not dare to send him to the city for provisions so I went myself. We did not need food, but I wanted to ask someone at Headquarters to get him off my back and to send me somebody normal.

The Commander was at meeting, his deputy slept drunk on top of the battlefield map. The secretary plugged her nose, gave me a bar of soap and directed me to the showers. I found two drunken boys there, quarrelling about who had humped the secretary the previous night, and whether she was better from the front or from behind.

I showered in my uniform, collected our food rations and ammunition, bought a bottle of brandy and made my way back to the mountain. At least some kind of order seemed to exist up there.

I watched the moon wavering in the half empty bottle of brandy. Once upon a time, my mother had told me that I could die if I looked at the moon too long. If that were the case, I would have been dead a long time ago. Before the war, I worked in an observatory, spending more time on the moon than on earth.

I reached our trench some time before dawn. Lamb ran towards me. Turd sat in the middle of the minefield, wailing, surrounded by a heap of papers. I howled that he was an idiot, that he should get back right away before he got killed. I yelled across the minefield that I would have him court-martialled. He just kept wailing.

"Which way should I return?"

"What do you mean, which way, idiot! The same way you got there!"

"I don't remember," he said, and continued to wail.

Lamb explained what had happened. After I left, Guts started in on Turd, describing the sexual pleasures women tended to indulge in when they were far from their husbands. Guts told Turd how they often gave themselves to lawyers since they could not only work out their divorces but could also wring the property away from their former husbands. Turd responded with curses, of course. The other side loved the whole thing, and was obviously having great fun. Guts shouted that it was a pity that he did not know Turd's real name because he had a whole bunch of divorce applications on him. If Turd was interested, Guts said, he could read them himself. He flung a whole bunch of papers into the minefield.

The wind that used to carry from their side the odour of stinky socks or whatever they were cooking, now brought a couple of the papers straight into our trench, and Turd saw that they were indeed divorce applications.

Lamb did not know when it was that Turd covered half the distance between the two trenches, ending up in the middle of the minefield. He understood what was happening only after he heard Turd howling, after they started shooting from the other side. He saw what I saw: Turd in the middle of the minefield, howling and clutching documents in one hand, propping himself against the sign that said *Mine Field* with his other arm, bleeding profusely.

Lamb said that they had fired a few shots, more to scare Turd than anything else. They obviously found it more interesting to joke at his expense than to finish him off. Judging by the camera flashes I knew that this scene would be seen in other places. I cursed the war and trenches, the minefields and the fools. Lamb cowered in the corner of our trench and accepted my insults as his due. I tried to pull myself together and discover a solution, but the way things looked I could count on God's help alone.

Somehow, I fell asleep.

I don't know how long I fought the nightmares, but I woke up spooked by the silence. My head ached and an ugly nausea had settled in my stomach. Lamb sat by the dead fire, doodling in the ashes with a stick. Turd was still in the middle of the minefield, whimpering, a frozen dog. Only silence emanated from the other trench. I tried to figure something out but my brain was not working. All I felt was rage.

"Guts!" I shouted. "Why don't you kill him? Be a man and spare him this misery."

"Why don't you kill him?" Guts responded. "He's yours. We don't need him one way or another."

"The man will bleed to death. If you have any soul left, let me at least throw him some bandages."

"I am better than you think."

"Can we make a deal?" I pushed on, afraid of what I might be getting into. "Don't shoot. I will come out unarmed."

"Do as you please. No one will fire a shot from this side."

"Can I be sure about that?"

"If my word is good enough, you can."

I packed some bandages into a bag and cursed myself for trusting a man who had been trying to kill me for months. I deserved to be shot.

Lamb simply stared at me. If he'd said anything at all, I would have given up. He did not. I told him not to touch his rifle and that if they shot me he was under direct orders to leave immediately for Headquarters to tell them about the meritorious death of two idiots. I took a final swig of brandy and jumped out of the trench. I walked slowly towards the minefield, noxious, feeling bigger than I was. I wished my mother had given me birth as a dwarf. My steps felt too short, while the field that had bore witness to our bullets and insults grew increasingly enormous and menacing.

All that remained of Turd was a pair of bloodshot eyes and a muddy uniform. He looked straight ahead, unblinking, and would not answer me at first when I asked him where he was hit.

"In my heart," he managed finally, not looking up.

He was close to madness. I threw him some cigarettes and bandages: they fell all around him, within easy reach, but he paid no attention. I stood there nervously, my stomach churning, unsure of whether I should go or stay, what else there was I might say.

Suddenly, from the other side, Guts appeared. He was nothing like I'd imagined him. I had pictured a husky peasant, more familiar with a plough than a book, but he was tall, skinny and bearded, more like me with my weight of a concentration camp inmate than how I had imagined him.

"I thought that you would be more of a soldier, not so scrawny," he called, with a poorly concealed smile.

"I was totally wrong about you, too," I said, assessing the fastest way back to our trench.

"You know, no one is happy about what has happened to this wretch. Even though he is not on my conscience, I have sent a boy to Headquarters to find the blueprint of the minefield, or the one who laid the mines. That is all I can do. As for you, don't shoot any more. Some of you might get hurt." He laughed. It was his favourite joke. He also threw a pack of cigarettes at Turd. We took off to our respective sides.

I dropped into the trench and immediately grabbed for the brandy. My legs ached as much as if I had just walked several kilometres. Lamb did not even raise his head. I pushed the bottle into his hand. He was like an endlessly ashamed child. With darkness, sleet started falling. I checked on Turd with my flashlight; those from the other side did the same. He stared at the ground and smoked. We drank, not so much out of craving, but rather to forget the sickness that would not let us sleep.

Around midnight, Turd started singing. It sounded like a prayer at first, a prayer in both Serbian and Arabic, a prayer only Turd knew the meaning of. It sounded like a child's lament, then a prayer, then something much closer to wailing.

He would stop only to light another cigarette, and then go back to it again, in a raspy voice that made our hair stand on end. His voice getting raspier and weaker until, just before dawn, he lost it entirely. I went to check on him. The tracks in the fresh snow told me that someone from their side must have checked on him as well. His face was blue and he did not raise his eyes when I begged him to unpack the bandages and at least wrap them around the bloody sleeve of his trench coat.

I watched that miserable figure that had driven me to rage for months. Now I felt only guilt. Every word I could think of as potentially meaningful sounded stupid and hollow when squared with the fact that there was no way for me to help him.

Guts appeared on the other side, shouting that they had not yet found the soldier or his blueprints, but that there was still a chance that he might be found elsewhere.

"Doesn't anybody among you know the pattern?" I felt the terrain with a light foot.

"When they laid it down they gave all of us a leave," Guts called back nervously.

I turned to leave but stopped when I heard Guts explain to Turd that the documents that had dragged him into the minefield were forgeries printed by his Headquarters as part and parcel of the "special war," and that if he'd known that this would happen he would never have joked about it. I could not tell whether he was comforting Turd or apologizing. Then he said something that his Command would have had his head for—something I would not have expected to hear from him, whose voice I had hated for months, whose death I had repeatedly imagined, unrealized only because I'd not yet got my hands on him.

"I am not asking you to forgive me," he said. "By that

time, worms will be eating us all and everything will be forgiven. Had anybody asked me, this war would have never happened. I was pushed into it no less than you. Here, look, we are wearing the same uniforms. Only our flags are different. If this minefield was not here between us I would not be able to distinguish your soldiers from mine . . ."

He might have said something else, but he noticed that I was listening. He threw Turd another pack of cigarettes and went back to his trench. Turd never raised his head as Guts spoke. The hand he couldn't feel any more clutched a bloody piece of paper, one that appeared more important to him than the minefield.

We were all going mad. Left in the bush for months, scrawny, drowsy, with one single wish—to survive—we increasingly resembled ghosts. It had been a long time since I'd opened one of the few books I'd taken with me when I left home. I no longer read them; I only opened them when I needed some paper to roll a cigarette, or to use their pages as toilet paper. My favourite writers were gradually being reduced to covers. We pleaded with Turd for some time, asking him to sell us his prayer book as cigarette papers, but he refused. That book now lay on his canvas covered by a fine layer of snow, ignored by everyone.

Guts and I met again around noon, when the sun started to melt the first light cover of snow. He called out to me from a distant corner of the field, far away from Turd. I knew that he had bad news. The news was indeed bad: the man who planted the mines had been shot, executed by their firing squad a week earlier for subversion, and no one knew where the blueprints to his minefields were. Worse, Guts had received a direct order to end this farce because some foreign journalists had managed to get pictures of Turd in the mine-field. He was expected to send a dispatch to his Headquarters confirming that everything had been taken care of. We both knew what this meant.

"Talk him into running for it," Guts said, "and let him have whatever God grants him. If he makes it out, a weight will be lifted from our minds as well, because none of my men wants to kill him. If he refuses, you kill him. He's yours."

I cursed their minefield and Guts cursed the kind of army whose soldiers ran into minefields.

Turd did not respond when I called him again. Surrounded by cigarette butts, he stared at the cigarette burning between his fingers and mumbled something unintelligible. Half of his uniform was soaked in blood. I told him again to pull himself together, to take his chances and dash back to our line; I told him that it would be best if he did it now, while it was still daylight, so that we could take him to the city hospital right away. I told him that the mines were obviously planted by an incompetent quack who had made all kinds of mistakes—how else had Turd made it to the middle at all? I might as well have been talking to a wall. My words sounded hollow and senseless. I knew that what I was really doing was talking him into suicide.

I wanted to throw him a pack of cigarettes, but there were already several unopened packs lying around him. I gave up. I returned to the trench with the same nausea I felt when I left it. Lamb sat in a corner of the trench and sobbed. It had been a long time since we had cooked anything and our monthly ration of brandy was low.

I told Lamb that I was going off to chop some wood, took one of our last bottles of brandy, and went to the mountain meadow below our trenches where I used to go whenever I had no idea what to do with my time. Lying down, I stretched and listened to birds chirrup. Squirrels frolicked in the high branches of the trees. A foolhardy rabbit almost jumped into my lap, but I had no will to shoot. The sun and brandy intoxicated, penetrating my trench coat like tenderness, before retreating like vapour. I fantasized about a special helicopter unit arriving and extracting Turd from the minefield, Turd waving as he ascended. I fell asleep. I dreamt that Turd's bloody hand crawled under my pillow, and that I kept hiding from it in the most unlikely places: a morgue, a graveyard, on top of a skyscraper.

I woke up to a gun shot.

It was nearly dark. Lamb was so drunk that it took a couple of minutes to bring him to his senses, and then only to hear that he knew nothing, and that he'd not even heard a shot. I snapped, told him that he was useless. He continued to stare through me like an otherworldly drug addict. A flashlight cut the darkness from the other side of the field, circling around the spot where Turd should have been. I directed my own beam in the same direction. Turd lay by the sign marking the minefield, his head bloody, a cigarette burning low in the corner of his mouth. I stared at that stretched out body and felt nothing beyond bitter tobacco in a dry throat and the same nausea that had settled in my guts when this whole mess had begun. Yet there was also perhaps some sense of relief, tiny as a particle of sand.

"Good shot boys!" I cried out. "Straight in the head. Congratulations."

"Don't be a fool!" Guts, resonant, responded. "Nobody fired a shot from here."

"Then who blew his head off? A squirrel?"

"Ask Turd. He's the only one who knows." The wind carried Guts voice, raspy with exhaustion. "Just get him out of there as soon as possible, or we'll have some wolves and vultures on our backs."

I didn't believe that they hadn't fired the fatal shot. Turd rarely carried a weapon. He did not like them. His own issued revolver was where he'd left it, under several inches of snow with the rest of his belongings. I didn't believe he'd had another pistol I hadn't known about. Fuck it, I told myself, and left, flashlight in hand.

Turd lay with his eyes staring skywards. His face was pale and sunken; it looked as if he'd been dead for quite awhile. But the fresh blood he was lying in was evidence it hadn't been long. What we called "a lady's gun" lay near his body, a gun we'd often laughed about as an insult to real pistols.

"Fuck it," said Guts from the other side. "I feel sorry for him. God help him, but perhaps this is for the best. Now you can tell your people he died in combat."

"Something like that." I lit half a cigarette. I inhaled the smoke, desperate. "We'll pull him out tomorrow, as soon as it's light. We can talk then about the price."

"I don't deal in corpses!" Guts snapped. He told me that I must be stupid if I didn't understand that no one on their side had wanted this to happen. I told him that I was not stupid and then added something dumb about having been born a smart baby before someone mixed me up in the maternity ward. Suddenly, Guts was laughing: he held his belly with both hands and laughed. I was laughing with him.

We must have been a ghostly sight as we stood laughing, our flashlights dancing upon a dead man. Perhaps I used to

39

be normal, way back when. I used to take off into the bush to cry my woes out, then.

Guts advised us to make metal hooks and tie them to a rope to try to snag Turd like a fish and drag him to our side without looking out from our trench, so that the exploding mines would not blast out heads off. Lamb finally managed a fire, we took the handles off some water buckets, softened them in the fire and made a few hooks. Some time after midnight we ran out of rope so I asked Guts if they had any, and he threw us a bag with rope and a few packs of cigarettes. I told them we had something for them as well and threw a bottle of brandy from the edge of the minefield. Someone on their side yelled and cursed because the bottle had apparently caught him pissing, but judging by the merry cheers coming from their trench later that night it appeared all was forgiven. One of them shouted that I should practice assassination attempts more often. Later on, one of their younger guards told a stupid joke and we all agreed that it was stupid and that if he got killed it would be for telling bad jokes.

It was as if an invisible weight had been lifted from our backs. Even the languid Lamb livened up, telling me how they pulled his brother from a frozen lake in a similar way. I did not ask whether his brother was pulled out alive. That question belonged to another time. It was enough that he'd spoken, so I could stop feeling alone and avoid asking myself questions better left until later, when they might hurt less. We fell asleep with rope in our hands, without any agreement about who would stand guard when. It started to snow.

❖ ❖ ❖

At dawn we were startled awake by a deep growl. I jumped up, peeked out from our trench and stood, frozen. In the middle of the minefield a huge grey bear struggled with Turd's body. He'd dragged Turd a few metres already, and was now resting. By the tracks in the snow it was obvious that the bear had tramped through the entire field at least a couple of times before he tried dragging the corpse away. He had tramped through the field a couple of times, and no mines had exploded. It could mean but one thing. I was immediately sick. Then I freaked out.

I grabbed my machine-gun, jumped out of the trench, and started shooting at the bear like a madman. He tried to run to the other side of the field as I changed my clip, but Guts and his soldiers opened fire from over there. Beside me, Lamb screamed and fired, completely out of his mind. We fired at the bear, entranced, desperately pouring out all of the bitterness, misfortune and rage that had settled within us.

We kept firing. Bullets tore into the bear's flesh. The bear finally rose up on his hind legs, as if trying to climb into the sky, and showed us his enormous, bloody figure. He moaned, a last, strangled roar, stretched his body out on top of the sign marking the minefield, and died. Our guns smoking, engulfed by a gunpowder mist, we stood and silently watched as life gushed from the forest giant in ever shorter breaths.

We stood facing one another. We could shoot at them. They could shoot at us, too.

They took their helmets off and crossed themselves as I entered what we knew as the minefield and dragged Turd's corpse to the trench. He felt very light. I could hear Lamb's teeth chatter as he followed the bloody trail left in the snow.

Before wrapping him up in a piece of canvas I worked open the stiff hand which still firmly clutched a piece of paper. It was a divorce application, though it was not from his wife. I stared at that crumpled piece of paper soaked in blood, and I could think of nothing. In this piece of canvas lay the real corpse of a real man who lost his life in a fake minefield, running after a forged document. I wondered whether we were real armies or whether we were just poor actors in a bad drama performed for an unseen audience.

Yet we had lost ourselves so much in our reality play that we'd even forgotten our own names, and called one another by nicknames we never chose, names given to us by our enemies.

It would have been so nice if Turd could have stood up and wiped off his make-up, if we could have taken down the props, sighed in relief and gone home to sweet jam-filled doughnuts and our even sweeter children, lazily getting ready for school. But Turd never moved, not when I threw the bloody paper into the fire, nor when I tied his hands and legs with a rope, or even when I moaned with the pain that ripped through my intestines.

I had to pay some gypsy to take Turd's body back to the city. I also sent a letter to Headquarters, describing recent events. A young captain arrived with twenty soldiers before nightfall, with an order for me to pack up my things and report to Headquarters with Lamb immediately. I wanted to tell him what had happened, but he turned his back on me. We didn't say goodbye when we left.

Back at Headquarters, my own captain cursed me and

called me a traitor, even though there was a time when he naively thought I might earn a medal. He threatened to have me shot, then promised to have me locked up in prison for having collaborated with the enemy. He bought me a drink in the end, and told me I was being transferred to the Headquarters' guards. Turd's case ended up in a file titled "Heroic Death."

I couldn't have cared less.

I wanted to tell him how it had all happened, but he wouldn't listen. He told me that he'd burned the report I wrote about the events at Black Hill, and then walked out of the canteen. Lamb and I went on drinking until dawn and then went our separate ways. I was later told that Lamb was on duty the night the arsenal blew up. His case was put in a file labelled "Disappeared."

Speaking of Black Hill, I heard only that our replacements pulled back to our old positions, not due to the enemy's advance but because the bear's corpse started rotting. It was the suffocating stench that drove them back, nothing more.

❖ ❖ ❖

Later, I ran away from the war, and dreamt of a time when I would wake up without a pain in my guts.

I gradually started to forget about it all until I saw Guts, just the other day, here in Toronto.

I was coming back from the doctor who had examined me for the umpteenth time, and tried to convince me once again that there was nothing wrong with my stomach and that nothing ails me. I was on my way home, when I saw a man sleeping underneath a maple tree. I recognized Guts right away. He was sleeping with some crutches by his side, his trouser legs empty. By the crutches was a little cardboard box upon which someone had scribbled *Please help a victim of war*. On top of his belly rocked an empty wine bottle, while beside him squirrels kept insolently filching pieces of a sandwich he had not managed to finish.

He was breathing hard, and moaning. I sat down and waited for him to wake up.

I wanted to ask him whether he was the one who threw that little lady's gun to Turd and whether he'd ever suspected that the minefield between us was fake. I needed to know if he ever met Turd in his dreams, because he never left mine. So I waited, while Guts whined in his sleep.

After a while, I went to the liquor store and bought a bottle of brandy. When I returned Guts was gone. There was no trace of him. The grass was not even pressed down where he'd slept.

That nausea was back in my stomach again.

I opened the bottle, sat down against the maple tree and started to drink. It feels like I am sitting there still.

ANOTHER BEAR

I WOULD NEVER HAVE GUESSED that the war had come so close, had I not gotten stuck at a bus terminal in a small town in the Bosnian countryside. The bus for Sarajevo was parked at the platform, but the driver was nowhere in sight, even a half hour after we should have departed. Taxicabs with no drivers were parked all around, shops were open with no vendors. A panhandler had departed in a hurry, leaving behind his cane and a hat full of change.

"The driver is at a meeting," a fat cashier said, continuing to embroider a flag I had never seen before.

"They're all at the meeting, it'll end when it's over, and you can wait in the tavern," she said, and pointed with her thumb over her shoulder.

She seemed to despise anyone not at the meeting. Underneath the unfinished flag there was a hole in her sock.

It was in this tavern, where half-empty beer bottles littered the tables, that I solved the riddle I'd carried with me ever since childhood. A bored Gypsy sitting on his accordion case in the corner gave me the answer as he waited for the patrons to return. He did not know what the meeting was about, and said that he did not give a damn about flags and their peoples. He was happy that Gypsies had no state, so that they had no reason to worry about it.

"Good times," he complained, "are long gone." He was forced these days to play in the cafes for small change instead of making good money in the open farmers' markets. There

45

were no such markets any more, and most of the Gypsies had moved to Italy, sensing the coming war. I plied him with beer and uncovered the details that had preoccupied my boyish imagination such a long time ago.

As a boy, I had been fascinated by the sight of the great Bosnian bear—the undisputed master of the forest, at whose mention shepherds froze—obediently dancing on its hind legs in front of a little Gypsy boy beating a drum.

My uncle, strong as a bull and often heated by powerful home-brewed brandy and the flaming glances of his fiancée, once bet in the tavern that he would wrestle such a bear in the morning. The next morning, when the betting party arrived to pick him up, he was already on the bus to Sarajevo, allegedly due to an urgent business affair that could not wait.

The little Gypsy boy beating his drum was so poor and unimpressive that he could have been forgotten the moment he picked up his coins had he not had his secret. I can still remember his contemptuous glance after I offered him my new shoes and my grandfather's ham for it. I did not know at the time that some secrets are not for sale.

But times have changed, and most secrets now have their price. I learned that the crafty gypsy hunters would steal a newborn bear cub and run away with it as fast as they could, fearing the mother bear, who would desperately follow their track until she went mad with sorrow and slaughtered the first flock of sheep she stumbled upon.

The rest was routine.

They first drove a hole through the cub's nose and passed a ring through it so it could not run away. Next, they forced the cub onto a sheet of metal, red-hot from the fire burning beneath, holding him so that he could not go free. As the bear hopped in pain, the Gypsies beat their drums.

Six months of this painful ritual would make the cub start getting up on its hind legs, understanding that it is less painful to hop on two legs than on four—the beat of the drum now its invitation to dance. Teaching it to bow after someone had thrown a coin into the hat was simply a matter of nuance, taught on the same red-hot metal, at a different drum beat. Moving from one farmers' market to another, the bear would get used to living with the Gypsies, forgetting the forest, that ancient native land it never grew to know.

When I was older, the authorities banned such abuse to protect the bears. They put the wandering Gypsies under control. No village their wagon trains passed through was left untouched. The Gypsies were good merchants, and even better thieves. There was a saying: before trading with Gypsies, swallow your wallet, and think about the deal until the morning. The bears were just a distraction.

"You have no idea how much I loved my bear. All my children learned to walk with its help. I left him in the deep forest ten times, and ten times he came back."

The Gypsy was in tears.

"Imagine. The last time I took him to the forest I fired a shot above his head. He stood up and started to dance."

That year the hunters' associations banned the bear hunt because it was embarrassing to shoot at animals walking upright. The hunters were also embarrassed to acknowledge that they shared their lunches with the tame forest bears.

A bunch of men burst into the tavern, talking loudly. The Gypsy started unpacking his accordion, and I ran towards the sound of the bus engine revving at the terminal. I jumped like a bear to a drum.

47

Halfway to Sarajevo, I noticed that my wallet was missing. "You paid well for your secret," I said to my reflection in the bus window. We drove through a thick forest. I kept thinking that it was indeed better not to know some secrets.

❖ ❖ ❖

At one point in my life, I used to make pocket money working at the Sarajevo Zoo. I worked as a guide on the weekends and cleaned the cages on work days. I often helped Kanada, a Gypsy woman in charge of cleaning five of the cages: the foxes, wolves, bears, lions, and tigers. I would start with the last three cages, hose in hand, after Kanada locked the animals up in the spare cage. I wore a gas mask; the terrible stench made my eyes burn. Another saying: you will wake up after sleeping with a fox only if you are a fox yourself.

Kanada was perhaps fifty, dark skinned and tall. She was likely beautiful once, before someone left a big scar across her forehead. And her name? People used to say that she was named after her father—a Canadian soldier serving in Italy after the Second World War. Others said that she had never married, because she fell in love with a Canadian tourist and promised to wait for his return.

Whatever the truth of the matter, she wore a windbreaker, winters and summers, with a small Canadian flag sewn to the back. She was always sombre. The only time I ever saw her smile was when she was working with the bears. She entered the cage as if there was nothing to it, talked gently in her gypsy tongue, and the bears would lie down on their backs and breathe loudly while she scratched them behind their ears.

One evening, after closing time, I saw her lying on the concrete floor, looking at the stars through the cage bars. Beside her lay a couple of bears, one on each side. Seeing her unmoving eyes, a bit of her body showing between the great beasts, I ran to the night guard, and told him that Kanada was in the cage, crushed by the bears. He waved me away and continued to watch his television. Kanada, he explained, was the last person the bears might hurt.

"Did you not notice," he said, "that she's more of a bear than a human being?"

Eventually, I got used to such things. I no longer thought it strange when she christened a newborn bear cub Son; nor that she was the only zookeeper the mother bear allowed to take her cub to show to children. I don't know whether I have ever seen someone pamper a baby as gently as she pampered that bear cub.

Our manager was a swine, and cared more about the money to be made through ticket sales, the merry- go-round and the pinball machines, than he did about the animals. He told me that he only hired Kanada because the Yugoslav authorities insisted on jobs being created for the Gypsies.

"Kanada," he used to say, "is the only one among them who lives in a high-rise flat and does not lift up the parquet flooring and burn it in the middle of the living room like all the other Gypsies who were showing the authorities how much they missed the confiscated tents and wagons."

I knew he was telling a half-truth, but I said nothing. I was in love with his daughter, Julia. She was my first love. She was the only other person allowed to watch Kanada stare at the stars, surrounded by bears. This gave me a chance to caress her breasts, that did not resist my fingers. I did not know it

49

then, but she would marry another night guard a few years later, and live in a house by the fence of the zoo. I thought she deserved more, back then.

She was the only one I told a secret that seemed as big as the sky. One summer night I took her to the bear cage and started rhythmically beating on the metal plate with the bears' names on it. Two forest giants appeared, looming mountain-high on their hind legs. They clumsily swung about to the rhythm of my beating, apparently not noticing the cub running between them all confused, growling for attention. Their eyes were turned skywards. Nothing else existed for them but the sound and memory.

I have no idea how long I beat on that plate. I thought only of Julia's laughter. The bears must have bowed when the silver bracelet fell off Julia's wrist as we ran towards the tall grass to hide from the searching flashlight of the night guard. The bears retreated deeper into their cage, as if nothing had happened; the stars remained fixed in the sky.

Later that night, Julia started crying, as if she understood more than I could gather. I understood only that my big secret had ended in tears. I would often show the same thing to other girls, later on. I made up stories about the long months I spent taming those ferocious forest beasts, which had, of course, often tried to attack me.

Then one night, as I beat on the plate, Kanada appeared, a terrible expression of disgust and rage on her face. She would probably have strangled me with her bare hands had my girlfriend not screamed. As we ran away, she hurled curses at me.

"A day will come for someone to remind you of something you will want to forget," she screamed as I scrambled for the exit.

I never went back to the zoo. The manager kept sending me messages saying everything was fine, and that I should pay no attention to Kanada's demand that I apologize to the bears. The summer had already gone anyway. I never went back, mostly out of fear of Kanada.

The last I heard about the zoo came from Julia. Some time in the middle of the war I recognized her in a long line of people, waiting at the semi-destroyed bus terminal, desperately believing that the announced bus would arrive and take them out of the city. I was the driver who came to tell them that they were waiting in vain. She was pregnant then, and still lived in the house by the zoo. The zoo unfortunately found itself in a no-man's-land between the rebels and our army.

She told me the zoo was no more. All of the animals had either been killed by the shells, let loose from the cages, or died of starvation. Only the released nightingales and the parrots, which never flew farther than the next tree top, were left as a reminder of the former animal kingdom.

"The sharpshooters have moved into the cages," she said. "May God leave them there after they have spent their ammunition."

She told me the unbelievable story about how Kanada and the bears had met their end. During those first six months of the war, when nobody could sleep at night because of the howling of the animals starving in their cages, Kanada was the only one who dared to go and feed them. Every night, she would fill bags full of food and crawl through the tall grass to the cages. Sometimes she made three trips a night, and the neighbours knew which animals had been fed when their howling stopped. She said the rebel snipers hidden behind the monkey cages wasted more bullets on Kanada than on the Bosnian soldiers. Kanada made only one mistake. She rose up for a second to scratch Son through the bars. The bullet went straight through her heart, yet she managed to crawl to the gate and open the cage door. She died there.

"But the bears . . ." Julia said. She shuddered. "They looked at Kanada lying dead in a pool of blood . . . then the two bears stood up on their hind legs and smashed their heads against the bars until they crushed their skulls and died."

Julia turned to leave, but then added something else.

"Imagine. While the bears were smashing their heads against the bars, the little bear, Son, rose on his hind legs and started a funny dance. The way Gypsy bears used to dance in country markets."

❖ ❖ ❖

Three years later I left besieged Sarajevo and promised myself that I would live my life as if that war had never happened. I would take a job as a city bus driver and smile at the people as if I had never driven the dead and wounded. Sirens would not remind me of war alarms and I would never run panic-stricken to a shelter again. I would have in my apartment only a small pocket mirror that could not accommodate a whole face, so that I would not be able to see the deep shrapnel scar across my forehead. Nor would I care how much hair I have after the war. I took with me a single album with photographs taken before the war. Accidentally, one war-time photo got in there: it showed Vera and me burning books in a kitchen stove. I took the photograph out of the album and flung it out of the bus window. I wanted no reminder that Vera had been killed.

I sat in a bus terminal in a small southern Italian town whose name I can hardly remember. Across the street, the blue summer sky bathed in the laundromat window. The window advertised clean clothes in two hours, but when I dumped the few clothes I'd managed to take with me on to the counter, the owner told me that it would take four hours after all. He charged me in advance.

"You have just time enough to see a football game. Our guys are playing against Rome today. No man should miss that."

I liked the way he used the words *our guys*, and how he incautiously exempted himself from the company of men.

I will go see the game, I told myself. I will be with our guys. I will buy myself a team flag and become one of the guys having fun. I will curse the referee, I will whistle at every fault made by Rome, I will learn our team's anthem and scream when we score a goal. I will be a fan who goes to drink with other fans, analyzing the match at the top of my lungs. I will just be a fan among other fans.

I waited patiently in the long line for tickets. I bought a flag. I smuggled a bottle of brandy in the leg of my pants, and I sat at a place where our flags were most numerous. A man waving one of the biggest flags did not hide his disdain when I sat among them, and began yelling at me. I could not understand a thing he said, so I took out the brandy bottle and offered him a drink. He laughed and drank out of my bottle. Later on they all laughed and patted me on the shoulders. A guy covered in hundreds of tattoos gave me a fan scarf. I jumped off my seat when those in front of me jumped and I whistled when they whistled. I could barely see one corner of the field, largely hidden by the huge flag in front of me, so I had no need to ask what was the colour of our team's uniforms.

It is not the same football stadium where we used to bury our dead. That stadium does not exist anymore, I told myself. I don't believe I have ever seen such a beautiful red sun as that setting behind the stadium walls. It is not even close to the colour of blood flowing down the sewers after the rain.

When the bottle was half empty, our flags suddenly sagged, and there was sorrow where there had only a minute before been singing. The opposing team had scored a goal. Different flags went up and the other team's fans now jumped up and down, showing us their middle fingers. Perhaps they would have calmed down had our guys not started throwing bottles at them. They responded by throwing firecrackers. As the first one exploded near me, that old nausea returned and I dove between the seats, the team flag covering my head. I kept telling myself that they were not shells and that the war was long over for me, but my body shook terribly, just like it did the day they were bandaging my head in a blood-soaked street.

When I finally got back up on the feet that had refused to lift me up for who knows how long, our guys were still standing around me, but the magic had left their faces. Some snickered, others' gazes filled with reproach. Still others seemed to blame me for the goal. The tattooed fellow took back his scarf, disgusted at how wet it was with sweat. I wanted to tell them something, but instead of my own voice I could only growl, like the growl one could hear beneath the Gypsy tents a long time ago.

I left the stadium, having forgotten the flag, which for a brief moment had appeared to belong to a world I'd inhabited long ago. I went back to the laundromat, listened to the renewed chants and songs of the fans. When I looked at the laundromat shop window, I did not see myself in its reflection.

There, on the bench, sat a man who moved his finger across a map spread over his knees, a strange man searching on a map for a place and a country where New Year's Eve is so deserted that even a wild bear could pass through the city without being noticed.

A STORY ABOUT SOIL

MY FATHER WELCOMED the end of the Second World War with a Russian machine-gun in his hands and a five-pointed star on his military cap. The German fascists who had left behind fresh graves and burned houses had called him a "Crazy Bosnian," not wanting to call him "brave" or "stubborn" or "suicidal." It seemed not far from the truth. Nine bits of shrapnel remained under his skin which he never wanted removed. During the four years of the war he grew so old that when he came back even his townsmen hardly recognized, in his coarse soldier's face and grey hair, the jolly twenty-year-old who had been famous for his guitar playing, carousing, and breaking of women's hearts. No one knew when father's boyish face had taken on its frozen military expression.

It probably happened during the middle of the war when my father learned that his only brother, Vojin, was fighting on the side of the occupying army. Vojin the traitor, the family disgrace. I can see my father's shamed face harden, deep in the forest with his hundreds of soldiers, planning his next attack upon German positions. It could not have been easy to be the general of an army which joked about his brother behind his back. I am surprised my father didn't hang himself out of shame.

His fellow soldiers claimed that he would interrogate German prisoners all night in order to find out about Uncle Vojin. No one ever knew a thing. The truth was that Vojin wandered the forests with a dozen volunteers like himself, frightening peasants with stories about the evils of communism. Father sent angry messages into the void, saying that he would hang him on the family's old pear tree the moment he laid his hands on him.

Uncle Vojin, only a year younger than my father, was an obedient and quiet man who adored and admired his brother as a copy does an original. Vojin joined the Germans not because of his own beliefs, but due to the influence of my cunning grandfather. Wishing to preserve his estate and not certain which side would win, grandfather made him join the Germans so that one of his sons could return victorious and preserve the family house and property. Secretly, grandfather helped both sides with food and wished for the war to end in a draw. When Vojin's forces were defeated, grandfather pretended he had wanted that all along, and cursed Vojin as a family disgrace. At the end of the war, uncle hid for a while in the forests far from the family estate, so he never heard about the amnesty. One day Uncle Vojin vanished, knowing that father would never have allowed an amnesty for him.

At a ceremony held in honour of the war heroes, father accidentally touched the arm of the woman who was helping him pin his medal properly. A month later he married that woman, and I came to love that woman as my mother. That was the time when father, then a retired officer, could hardly stand peace. He had terrible nightmares. He moaned and gave orders in his sleep. He crawled all night from one corner of the room to another, and woke up more tired than when he'd gone to bed. Several years after the war, dreaming that somebody had thrown a bomb into the room, he jumped out the window and broke his leg. After that he calmed down, started keeping bees, and began to notice his two sons.

Nobody spoke about Vojin. When his name was mentioned, it was in a half-whisper, as when you speak of a family disease. Father diverted our curiosity by claiming that he'd disappeared some time during the war. He never spoke his name. Uncle Vojin's picture disappeared from the family album, replaced only by a grey layer of hardened glue. Growing up, we learned what we knew about Vojin from grandfather, who, before saying a single word would make sure father was not around. We grew up with uncle's ghost, or rather with the ten-year-old Vojin in the only picture my grandfather had managed to keep. In that picture, Vojin sat beside father with a melting ice cream cone in his hand. As he gazed at the picture, we could see the pain in grandfather's face.

Ten years later, when grandfather failed to wake from his afternoon nap, we found dozens of Vojin's letters under his pillow. They were sent from Canada to grandfather's secret post office box in the neighbouring town. Vojin said he'd forgiven grandfather long ago for guessing wrong in the war, and that he wasn't troubled by it any more. We would sneak into the cellar to re-read these letters whenever we had the chance, until father discovered them and locked them in the safe. Our shrewd grandfather knew that those letters would sooner or later fall into our hands, and today, when I think about what followed, I am certain that he destroyed some of that secret correspondence. It seems to me that later events happened exactly according to those missing letters.

Not long after we buried grandfather, a letter from Vojin arrived addressed to father. Mother, a gentle and quiet person, gave father such an angry look when he refused to read it that he sat down and reluctantly opened the letter. Uncle Vojin apologized for the disgrace he had brought upon the family and agreed that he deserved to hang from the pear tree, but said that it was too late because his days were numbered. His only wish, he wrote, was for his brother to send him a bag of soil from the garden, so that he could at least die smelling the soil he would never see again. He would, in return, send father Canadian soil. Father threw the letter in the furnace and went to tend his bees.

A few days later a man came to our door with a bag of soil on his shoulder. Since the foreigner spoke only English he didn't understand my father, who complained that Vojin was an incorrigible fool for sending him capitalist soil and trying to disgrace him in front of the neighbours. Father ordered us to throw the Canadian soil into the creek and to fill the empty bag with soil from the garden in order to get rid of the foreigner before the neighbours noticed.

That was the only bag we ever emptied into the creek. All the others that followed we emptied in father's garden. When we threw out the contents of that first bag, photographs and paper money surfaced on the water. I don't know if mother knew the secret of our frequent visits to the basement. We would go there not to count the currency, the value of which we did not know, but because of the postcards with images of Hudson's Bay, igloos and Niagara Falls. Above all, we studied Uncle Vojin's photograph. He was tall and lean like death, and stood in front of a huge house. He stared straight ahead, like a convict. He was alone. In the background we counted twelve cows, and proudly concluded that uncle was now rich.

Father was not any kinder to the next courier, a tanned

young man with the look of a sailor, and concluded that these Canadians must be primitive people since they didn't speak Serbo-Croatian. He started writing angry letters telling uncle to leave him alone, but mother kept reminding him that his brother was dying, and that she would never forgive herself for denying his last wish. We would immediately grab the bags and wait for father to withdraw to his bees in order to check the contents.

As Vojin's death was prolonged, father stopped getting angry when unannounced visitors brought and took away soil. He only got angry at the moles which burrowed into the garden whenever my brother and I filled the empty bags. Father took pride in his garden. Friends would come from far away just to taste that strange savoury pink potato which grew only in his garden.

As time passed, father became less partisan, and only remembered the war when the weather changed and the shrapnel in his back started to sting. He stopped retelling the same old war stories, though he would sometimes tell stories from his childhood with Vojin after a few brandies. We pretended to listen, although we often knew them from the letters Vojin sent in the bags of Canadian soil.

Everything changed that spring Bosnia started falling apart. Prostitutes turned into psychics overnight and became too expensive. Local fools with flags in their hands and pistols tucked under their belts entered our house and left with bottles of plum brandy. Father would nod his head at everyone, see them off with a smile, then go out to his garden or to tend his bees. He intended to cut the old pear tree in the yard, because it was so old that it had started leaning on the house, but he didn't have the strength any more.

Vojin's bags of soil stopped arriving. The bags had come for so long that father hadn't noticed when mother put Vojin's picture back in the family album. Nor had he noticed how quickly he had grown old. He was hardly aware that his own sons were now men, nor how different we had become, and that Vojin's secret was the last real bond between us.

It was long enough for us to know that Vojin's money might buy two plane tickets.

Mother said she would explain everything to father on the plane.

I arrived at the airport from a political meeting. Brother arrived at the last moment, from who knows where. When father embraced him, I noticed my brother's right shoulder hurt him. This always happens when a young soldier first learns to fire a rifle. Father whispered something in his ear for a long time, while I promised mother that I would look after my brother. When he embraced me, father didn't whisper a thing. The plane took off quickly.

Only one letter arrived from Canada, a few days before our nightmares became reality. Houses in the neighbourhood were burning, refugees were roaming and looting the gardens at night, and I was sleeping with a pistol under my pillow. Mother addressed the letter to both of us, not knowing that my brother hadn't been home for months, and that the last thing he told me was that the homeland wouldn't be proud of me. I told him that my homeland was the family house, the garden, and the old pear tree. After that somebody wrote *traitor* on the wall of our house.

Mother wrote that Vojin had no intention of dying soon. Her only concern was that Vojin and father often quarrelled while working in the garden. Father claims that Vojin's

Canadian garden will never bear such pink potatoes as the ones back in Bosnia, while Vojin counters that there is not a single grain of Canadian soil in his garden, but that it consists entirely of Bosnian soil which he has spent all his money on to import. Father doesn't believe him and they fight until mother invites them in for lunch. Then they reminisce about their childhood.

She even sent a photograph.

Two senile old men sit in the garden, talking about soil.

God forbid, she wrote, the two of you become like them.

THE STORY OF SINAN

Remembering is not a disease . . . remembering is not a disease . . .
I repeat this to myself, rummaging amongst the old photographs. They are the only things I managed to save from my burned out apartment. Everything else was destroyed. Only wind and ashes remained. Besides myself, who no longer lives there.

I don't know when I last fell asleep before dawn. I spend part of the night watching what remains of the Don under the bridge. They say that it used to be a river. Now it is a dirty, nondescript creek. I spend the other part of the night gambling at the casino. The two parts of the night are separated by a chasm. Me.

My name used to be Jovan. I am called John now. These two names are also separated by a chasm. From time to time, I'm startled by the Kid's ravings, sometimes so clear that I can tell what's happening in his dreams. I have taken him to dozens of doctors, but their verdict is always the same: there is no damage. The boy simply refuses to speak. He only ever speaks in his dreams. He expresses himself through drawings. Ana, a Puerto Rican woman I hired to look after him, claims that she's deciphered his entire life through his drawings. When I ask her what she has deciphered she turns away in anger. If I were not paying her well she'd probably tell me I'm a bad father. She comes every morning and looks after the Kid the whole day. She tells me that some neighbours think she's my wife. God forbid. I was married once. Never again.

I open the album to the smell of burned ceiling beams and say to myself, it's good that you got out, you saved your skin. And the photos tell me its good you saved us because we'll last longer than you will. Photographs know how to deal with memory.

One photo shows Sinan and me lining up for water. I'm carrying a jerry-can. The photo is so clear I can smell the chlorinated water, the stench of months of uncollected garbage. Sinan is smiling, in a perfectly white shirt and navy blue jacket. I'm the thin-moustached man in the *Still alive in Sarajevo* T-shirt threatening a kid who tried to jump the queue. I got that photo from a French reporter who couldn't use it. A long line of pale, dirty people stare resentfully at the photographer. Sinan looks like someone who woke up a few minutes before in a warm hotel room and joined us in line to amuse himself. He has no jerry-can.

This was in the first year of the war. At the time, every citizen of Sarajevo hated the global TV crews and reporters who studded the city like vultures, following the smell of blood and sensation. We thought it all a brief, private nightmare that the world had nothing to do with.

Sinan moved into the attic apartment across from mine a couple of months before the city was besieged. It was a time when every reasonable person was packing suitcases and fleeing the city. My wife had left with the last refugee convoy. Soon afterwards, she wrote to me from Sweden asking for a divorce. War sometimes has a human face.

It was said that Sinan was an international gambler. In an earlier incarnation he had been a dentist. Everyone talked about him. Nobody knew who was sending private planes for him, or whether the two beautiful blondes in the hotel lobby resulted from a winning bet. He'd disappear for a few days, and not even the hotel spies could track his disappearances. When he resurfaced, no one could tell from his poker-face whether he'd won or lost.

Sinan stuck fast to his principle never to gamble locally, which was humiliating to local gamblers and gossips. Then the two blondes disappeared from the hotel unnoticed, followed by the red convertible. No one noticed: they had something more important to talk about.

The war had started.

The only person Sinan was seen with was his mother, my former history teacher, a cold and haughty woman who lived across the hall. I helped her take out her suitcases a few days before Sinan moved in. She told me he'd arranged for her to leave the city in a UN armoured vehicle. Her pension and a villa on the coast were waiting in Spain. With scorn she noted that Sinan had even gambled away his old love. She'd been waiting for him at the altar but he didn't want to interrupt a poker game. He'd lost everything.

Sinan moved in when the guns were unleashed and thundered so much that even the last birds moved out of the city, leaving it to be raided by grasshoppers. These were all over the city, some the size of sparrows. Men joked that these were male grasshoppers because they kept hopping under women's skirts until the last woman switched to pants. This was funnier than the gambler who'd been feeding their idleness for years.

Sinan moved from the big screen to a small one, entertaining the people in our building. He moved in with two crocodile suitcases and immediately installed a thick armoured door and an alarm system, which proved useless. The alarm sounded with every flea or gnat and I was the first to pound on his door and ask him to turn it off. Though within a couple of days things had taken care of themselves. The power supply to the city was cut.

He resembled neither a dentist nor a gambler, though perhaps a charming aristocrat unused to lifting anything heavier than a champagne glass. For those in his apartment block he made up for the lack of television by leaving his door ajar. Sinan's programs were mostly comedies. We laughed for days about the good looking woman he drove out of his apartment, the one who had not wanted to leave after he won her at cards, so much had she enjoyed her humiliating captivity. Then there was the episode about the twins, who had showed up together at his door one morning to clarify which of the two he should marry. Sinan pulled at his hair and cried that he had thought they were the same person, and that he felt cheated by their conspiracy.

Sinan was a wonderful and generous liar. He told women he wanted nothing to do with that huge rats had settled in his apartment, or that he had been diagnosed with syphilis. Perhaps the loveliest lie of all was that his wife had been unexpectedly released from prison, although she was supposed to serve five more years for murdering his ex-mistress.

In the war's first December, when hunger crawled into every apartment like vermin and hordes of refugees attacked and plundered anything that remotely smelled like food, Sinan appeared at my door to borrow a cup of oil. I invited him to dinner, fairly certain that he'd never cooked in his life. He did not look like a man who, even when driven by hunger, would hurt his manicured fingers by opening a can.

"You look like a man just abandoned by his wife," he said,

smiling, looking at the mess in my apartment. But he ate my burnt beans, ravenous. After that, he appeared regularly at dinner, freshly shaven and smiling as if arriving at a royal reception.

At the time I was terribly lonely. I'd read in the daytime, suppressing the need to go out, where I could be hit by a sniper bullet from the other river-bank, or picked up by one of the uniformed gangs and sent to the front line. In the evenings, I watched from behind dark windows the bridge now divided by chicken wire, and imagined that I was a bird, though never a chicken.

I had nightmares, always the same ones: I ran along the middle of the bridge, soldiers shooting at me from both sides.

You couldn't tell, looking at Sinan, that the city was under siege and that the obituary columns in the newspapers were longer than the editorials. He would sleep until noon, come to lunch with his inevitable smile and a couple of cans of meat, and then retreat to his apartment for the afternoon. In the evening, after curfew, he would follow his secret paths to wherever it was he went at night. I never asked him where he went, though I did point out that after ten at night the police shot without warning at everybody who happened to be in the street.

"Fools and thugs should be killed," he said. "It's the very meaning of war."

Today, I am no longer certain whether he was at all interested in knowing who was shooting at whom, or if he cared for my explanations about why the city was besieged. Every discussion we started ended in his swearing at roughnecks who would not let him gamble with Parisian gentry, and made him lower himself with upstarts, peasants, and petty thieves.

I once asked him caustically where he would go if they let him leave the city. He didn't answer me. I can't remember if he ever gave a direct answer to any of my questions. He backed down as if confronted with the glances of someone peeking at his cards.

He changed his routine only once a month, on the thirteenth. That day he would open a bottle of cognac and empty it within an hour. I had never seen anybody drink this way. He drank with such effort that each mouthful produced a grimace. He would sigh and groan as if drinking pain itself, sweat dripping from his forehead. He drank as if squeezing into a narrow room only he could enter.

After emptying the bottle he'd sit for hours, relieved, looking through the window, and then disappear, staggering past his armoured door. The next morning the neighbours would come asking if Sinan had died, after they'd heard him all night moaning and howling like a wolf. Then he'd show up at noon in his white shirt, his smile the same as ever but with deep circles under his eyes, and ask me if I'd finally learned how to cook. It was on these days that he'd always bring something special like a piece of fresh meat or fish as an apology. I would, of course, accept. In times of hunger everyone becomes as tolerant as a hooker.

❖ ❖ ❖

That second December Sinan showed up carrying in his arms the lifeless body of a boy. One side of the boy's face was covered with frozen blood. At first, struggling with my own

70

nightmares, I wanted to push Sinan out. I was afraid his gambling had taken a perverted turn. But Sinan was not smiling and the bleeding boy was hardly breathing. I took off the boy's torn jacket by the stove, and struggled with the frozen shoelaces. Sinan told me that he'd found him by the locked staircase door, a victim of street gangs. He was seven or eight years old, at most, and his scratched arms and legs were nothing compared to the bruises on his back. Sinan turned his head away as I cleaned the boy's wounds, as if he'd forgotten that he'd ever been a dentist. The boy woke up for a second under the warm blankets, stared at Sinan's face and, before his hand managed to reach the bandage on his head, fell asleep. He was feverish the whole night and didn't wake before noon next day.

I had never had children, and found myself at a loss. We tried to make some compresses from odds and ends in my kitchen, but Sinan was so confused that he was more a nuisance than anything else. He spilled warm water over the stove, and then dropped the sugar bowl, which shattered. When I asked him to hold the boy's leg so that I could put on some vinegar compresses, Sinan shook all over.

"What are you putting on his legs," he asked, averting his gaze.

"It's a blend of owl's eye, bat's wings, and mouse ears. . . ."

I didn't finish. Sinan lunged into the bathroom and threw up. Lovely, I thought. Instead of one patient, I now have two.

During the night, the boy raved. From his broken sentences I inferred that bandits had set his house on fire and that he had tried to reach the city with his mother. They had tried to cross the frozen river at night but his mother had fallen through the ice. The boy hid in the cellar of a demolished house for two days. He kept mentioning a knapsack with photos and addresses. He'd struggled to survive in a city where you could get attacked for less than a child's knapsack.

The Kid woke up the next day and did not stop crying until Sinan appeared with a funny metal toy, a bear with a drum. At night, he continued to rave—or was it the truth?—about fire, ice, his mother's coat and his knapsack. He did not speak a word during the day; I never even managed to find out his name. I gave him markers and paper. He used only the black one.

Sinan noticed this and brought him a dozen black markers the next day. I unkindly asked him if he'd bring the boy a bomb if he sketched it. I scavenged some clothes from my neighbours and took the boy to see a doctor. The boy held my hand with both of his, and I pretended not to notice the wet spot spreading on his pants. The doctor, dark circles under his eyes, looked at the boy's wounds, shoved a few rolls of bandages into my pocket, and said what I'd already known: the boy would start speaking when he was no longer in shock. Then people brought into the doctor's office a bleeding man whose ruined arm dangled over the stretcher.

My God, I thought, how nice it is not to have to leave the apartment.

At the Red Cross, they ironically asked me if I happened to know a new means of looking for the close relatives of a boy who didn't speak and who had no first or last name.

In the city orphanage they snapped at me that the building was so crammed with children that some of them had to sleep in the principal's office. The best thing would be, the skeletal superintendent told me, to go see the state president and ask him why he hadn't built an addition to the orphanage before going to war. I told him to fuck off, both him and the president, and would have slammed the door if it had had a knob.

The police told me that in the past ten days over twenty bodies with no papers had been pulled from the river. If I wanted, they could give me a shovel and show me the way to the mass grave. I didn't reply. The cop, whose cigarette never left his mouth, looked as if he'd be happy to put me into a uniform and send me to the front. I held on to the kid's hand then as tightly as he held on to mine.

It seemed that the boy smiled when I took him back home. I was also relieved. I told him his room and board would be a drawing a day. Later that day he reached for the red marker.

I called him the Kid. The name stuck.

Sinan came in the afternoon, refreshed from a good night's sleep, and joked that I should be grateful for getting a son so cheaply. I told him that the human race existed, not only because contraception hadn't been invented early enough, but because having a child usually required two people.

"Well," he said, "there are two of us. We could be the predecessors of a new civilization made up of adopted children of unknown origins."

He said this bitterly and sat down to draw with the Kid. The next day he brought a dozen red markers.

I communicated with the Kid as if he were a fish in an aquarium. I knew he was angry when he sat in a corner of the room facing the wall. I knew that he was sad when I caught him staring through the window, often for hours, at the bridge over the frozen river. From his life on the other side of the river he brought with him the ability to kindle fire, the need to water house plants all of the time, a fear of darkness, and a fear of anyone who knocked on the door.

Sinan still slept till noon, came for lunch freshly shaven, always smiling, and stayed till evening. The boy adored him. He would sit for hours telling the Kid the most improbable stories from his journeys, and even Sinan probably could not tell truth from fiction. He would speak ardently about the world's most beautiful summer resorts and restaurants, about fruit cocktails on Cuban beaches, night fishing in Hawaii, and the huge lobsters of Prince Edward Island, and he described them so vividly that the room was enriched by his descriptions. If it wasn't for the fact that he eagerly ate my mushy rice every day, I would have thought that he'd just dropped in to see me and kill time until next summer. Each story ended with him winning a game, the prize either a house on the Spanish coast or a yacht in the Adriatic Sea, and donating it to an orphanage. It was a reminiscence of a lost time, long gone, when Sinan's luck had yet to leave him, but the Kid devoured every word and wanted more. When Sinan repeated stories and mixed up events, the Kid would angrily go to the corner and stare at the wall and Sinan would find excuses in his forgetfulness and the war.

I did not approve of him teaching the boy card games and gambling tricks, particularly when I saw the zeal in the Kid's eyes while shuffling cards and dealing them out to us with professional speed. I could read real ardour in his eyes. To be honest, after three months, I didn't win a single card game.

❖ ❖ ❖

The first year of the war Sinan gambled mainly with the UN soldiers who were idle most of the time, their only task being to show up in the street and count the dead after bombardments. Most of their money was spent on prostitutes or gambling. That year military rations were brought to Sinan's apartment, and he stuck to his superstition that you mustn't eat food won gambling, since each milligram consumed shortened your life by an hour. I though it stupid, particularly when I was running to the make-shift market early in the morning and swapping fresh meat for old cans. I couldn't allow him to trade by himself because he'd come back from the market like a man who had fallen from another planet.

Once he brought a battery-powered train, at a time when the price of batteries equalled gold; another time he brought a radio although the city had been blacked out for months. Then there was the canned meat whose expiry date had passed a couple of years earlier. He would bring home such useless things. When I went out I couldn't suppress the fear of the gangs who were capturing conscripts in the streets and delivering them to the police in exchange for the cops' tolerance about the stolen food they resold in the markets.

Essentially, I'm a coward.

Once, they picked up Sinan on the street and took him off for the mandatory three-day ditch digging on the first front line. Over there, a shovel meant the same as a gun since snipers from the other side of the river couldn't tell the difference. He returned a day later without a single callus. As a memento of his time digging ditches he brought a handgun. After seeing the Kid's eyes burn while he passed his finger over the cold barrel, I made Sinan take it back to his apartment. The next day a young soldier appeared at his door, crying and begging him to return him his handgun, otherwise they'd court-marshal him.

I'm sure that Sinan didn't know who was shooting at whom the next year either. He was coming home empty-handed more often, and he'd swear at the war and the idiots who invented it so that he had to gamble with roughnecks instead of Las Vegas gentry. I pretended not to notice that the gold chain was missing from his neck. The shirts he wore were still white, but now had frayed collars; only one button remained on his jacket. But his smile remained unchanged, the same as his rule never to forgive anyone a gambling debt. Sometimes I despised him for this. I knew that he had a heart of gold but also a stone-hard soul.

Sometimes loud arguments in the corridor made me come out and try to mediate in favour of a loser. I got involved for the last time when a guy on crutches begged him to return his gold pocket watch, the only memory of his father, offering a bicycle in exchange. I said that he should respect the fact that the youth's memories could not be measured by the plating on the watch. He said that gambling was more important to people than anything they gambled.

"You have no idea what gambling is," Sinan said. "It's like living in fifth gear. You'd better not sit down if you don't know the brake from the accelerator." Later on he told me I was naïve if I had thought that the boy's crutches were real, that the bicycle hadn't been stolen, and that the crying youth was a thief who'd mainly come to check the type of the lock on his apartment. I no longer came out when I heard arguing. Not even for the sake of a skinny old man who came for days asking for the family icon his son had gambled away.

That year hunger moved in so completely that even the few beggars disappeared from the streets, ashamed to beg when almost everybody looked like a beggar. I had already sold all the paintings from the walls. I swapped the pool table for a bag of flour. Books and shelves, the only things that remained, ended up in the stove. The Kid spent less and less time by the window staring at the river, sketched houses in flames less and less, and was increasingly trying to memorize the alphabet on the pictures I stuck to the wall over his bed.

A letter from Sinan's mother arrived with a reporter who managed to enter our besieged city. She sent it to me knowing that I would get it to Sinan. She wrote that she was moving out of Sinan's villa on the beach, which she had been forced to sell because of unpaid taxes. With the money that was left she had arranged to have the Spanish UN battalion take Sinan secretly out of the city.

"On March 1`4, at dawn, a captain named José will come to fetch him and I'm begging you to make sure that Sinan does not mess it up. Remind him that he cannot take with him anything larger than a travel bag," my history teacher wrote. "I am sending you $200 and pray to God nothing nasty happens to you." I tucked the money into my pocket and felt the urge to cry. Then I returned the money to the envelope. If God is the only thing that remained to me, then the money would be useful to Sinan, I thought, though not without pain.

It was the middle of February. Sinan was drinking more regularly. One morning he came with a bottle of bootleg cognac made of brown sugar and pure alcohol, and before he started diving into the bottle, I told him about the letter. He stared with the mild unchanging smile of a man who, walking across the heavens, has no time to spare on earthly matters.

"Old whore," Sinan muttered. "She thinks she only owes me that much." He waved his hand as if he was past caring about it. He wasn't even in the mood to tell the Kid another story. The Kid's favourite tale was the one where Sinan had once won a whole circus at cards and driven all the caged animals to the forest to set them free.

Sinan was Kid's hero. He never listened to my bedtime stories with the same attention. Once, when changing the bandage on his head, I noticed that the wound had healed and I told him that he didn't need his white cap any longer. He cried the whole day and wouldn't let me take his bandages off. I told Sinan about it, and he told the Kid a story about how he'd dreamt that he no longer had the bandage on his head and about how happy he was. The Kid took it off immediately. I was his duty, Sinan his entertainment. I kept Sinan away from the bottle until the Kid fell asleep, in order to tell him this was the unique opportunity to save both his and the boy's life.

"I ended my life a long time ago, so all is a gift to me anyway," said Sinan over the bottle. His eyes had become small and yellow. He had lost a lot of weight.

"The Kid will never recover from this horror," I argued, "and has a much better chance in any European orphanage than he does here. Even the rats are leaving." I did not tell him about the terrible sickness I felt at the thought of staying on alone. We were a kind of patched-up family in which I, with my broken marriage, fared better than the boy with his broken past and Sinan with his broken life.

"Would you really leave the Kid in an orphanage?"

"I don't know," I said. "But I would understand if you did it because of your health." He looked at me, and before he could ask me why I considered myself better than he, I told him about the cruel joke circulating that Sinan had a tumour, but a tumour that did not develop any further. He laughed, which was just what I needed to be sure he'd heard me. I told him that he could carry the boy out of the city. He corrected me, saying that I had probably meant to say "take."

I said that I had said what I meant. Since the boy was so skinny and thin, Sinan could carry him out in a big travel bag as personal luggage. He told me I was insane and I said that only insanity had a chance. I showed him a bag that I could pad with a blanket. I pierced air holes in the top. He didn't even want to look at it.

"Isn't there a safer way to get out of Sarajevo?"

"Yes," I told him. "In a coffin!"

He drank away the rest of the evening. I tried to read, but noticed Sinan occasionally lift his head from the glass to stare at the bag I pretended to have forgotten in the middle of the room.

"If this is the only way," he said, "then fine." He left with his bottle unfinished.

Over the next few days Sinan appeared only briefly, just to make sure that there was food. He'd bring a box of cookies, or nonsense like an electric meat-grinder or a new pair of children's shoes that were too tight for the Kid. Even his famous smile had disappeared, as if he had gambled it away. He became round-shouldered and his stories to the Kid became so garbled and unfinished that the boy would often get up and angrily turn to face the wall.

Two days before the appointed date, when I started getting nervous, fearing that he might gamble away this only chance, Sinan appeared at dusk. The Kid was waving to him from the bag, as if he was on a ship that was to set off to sea. I had spent days telling the Kid how Sinan would take him in the bag to a country of good people where there was no war, where all the animals lived freely, and where a child's only task was to play. I told him that the bag was actually a ship which would take him to Canada. I'd put him in the bag while I talked, and he'd sit inside and follow my fabrications with his eyes open wide. The minute I got tired of inventing the delights of the Promised Land, the Kid would jump out of the bag and go to his sulking corner. His favourite story was the one about Sinan owning a whole circus of animals, and how they would travel and tour the most beautiful cities in the world. He'd sit in the bag for hours then, even after I stopped talking.

Sinan looked at that tiny head smiling at him from the bag as if looking at the face of horror itself. I saw him tremble, and then he slid to the floor.

"You really think I can make it?" he asked, almost crying.

"Of course you can. It's only a two-hour journey to freedom."

Then, in the half-darkness, I noticed the big black bruise, his swollen and closed eye, as if somebody had split Sinan's face in two. I knew it was the way gamblers collected unpaid debts. I went to the window, took an icicle, crumbled it into a plastic bag, and gave it to him.

"I think it's high time you got lost anyway." He tried to hide a painful grimace when he put the ice on the side of his face that no longer belonged to him.

The Kid went to his corner, angry because Sinan wasn't paying attention to him.

Sinan shoved the keys to his apartment into my pocket. He looked through the window. He told me he had one more game, and that I had better keep the keys so that he wouldn't be tempted to bet the apartment. He said to consider it my own. It would be valuable after the war, when people would once again need apartments. I don't have to say how much this shook me up. He handed me the keys to his last fortress, the one that he'd guarded so jealously.

I'd never asked myself what my place was in his life. For me it was enough that I wasn't alone, because I knew that loneliness would kill me as certainly as hunger. It wasn't only poor people's food I shared with him. I also shared the loneliness that had infected our dying city like a disease. Thinking about being alone again, I comforted myself with the thought that I'd always been a lone wolf. It occurred to me that he had given me his keys so that I could divide my loneliness between the two apartments.

Sinan went to the Kid and hugged him long and hard, as if he was saying good-bye. He called out to me to be careful not to lose the keys and disappeared out the door. I noticed the bulge of the handgun under his coat, and knew something terrible was going to happen.

❖ ❖ ❖

Gunshots from the bridge startled me from sleep. I looked out the window and into the early morning sun and watched as a man jumped across the chicken wire and ran across the bridge, shooting into the air. Shots rang from both sides of the bridge; from our side, because they thought that the man was a fleeing spy, while those on the other side fired fearing an attack. With my eyes I followed him to the middle of the bridge, where he fell down, riddled from both sides. His last breaths could be seen in the December chill.

I knew that it was Sinan.

I don't know if this was the way he'd imagined his death, or whether he had started running across the bridge with a smile, at least on that side of his face that was left to him. But, huddled in the pool of his own blood, he looked ghastly.

In the afternoon a policeman came and asked if I had the keys to Sinan's apartment. I said I didn't and he said he'd return the next day with his team to break down the door. He asked if Sinan had ever cooperated with foreign agents. I said that I didn't know. I told him that we were neighbours, but that we weren't that close. He would probably have taken me and delivered me to the army had he not seen the boy sitting in the travel bag, drawing with red markers.

"I hope you're a bigger help to this kid than you've been to me," he said before he left.

That evening I shoved the photo album from my previous, burned out apartment into the travel bag, and moved into Sinan's apartment. There was nothing in the apartment except the bed, an empty wardrobe, and an odd-looking notebook where Sinan had written out card combinations. The numbers and symbols were unintelligible. Before dawn I pushed two sleeping pills into the Kid's mouth and, when he was completely out, put him carefully into the bag. Shortly thereafter, two Spanish soldiers with flashlights showed up and addressed me as "Sinan." One of them offered to take my bag. He must have thought that I was carrying the family gold because I would not part with it all the way to the border. When we crossed the border, the Kid started raving in his sleep so loudly that they stopped the APC and shouted at me in a language I didn't understand, though I knew what they meant. I shoved the $200 from the envelope into the hand of one of them and both fell silent. The driver started the engine again, and we continued on.

Some time later they told me to take the boy, who was still sleeping, out of the bag so that he wouldn't suffocate. The soldier gave me the $200 back.

"We're soldiers, but we're not scum," I understood him to say.

Half way to Zagreb the Kid woke up and would have cried all the way if the soldiers hadn't comforted him with chocolates from their rations. But he didn't let me embrace him until I told him that Sinan would arrive later, because he had taken another APC. Perhaps I should have told him the truth then.

In Seagram we were welcomed by my history teacher, tanned from the Spanish sun, surprised to see me instead of Sinan. When the soldiers took the boy to buy him shoes, I briefly explained to her what had happened over the past two years and how Sinan had ended his life in the middle of the bridge. She kept sipping her juice long after I'd finished my story. Her expression remained as stern as it had been in high school when she lectured on the fall of the Roman Empire. I don't know what I had expected! Tears, lamentations. Anything but this stoicism, confronted with the death of a son, a civilization's fall. I guess that is why I had never understood anything about history.

"You know, I'd have been more surprised if Sinan had

listened to me and got out instead of you," she said. I saw my skinny and wrinkled face reflected in her sun glasses. It wasn't me anymore.

She ordered another drink. There was still no sign of the Kid.

"There is no longer any point in keeping things secret. Sinan is not really my son. We adopted him after the last war. The baby of some poor soul who strayed into a minefield with her three other children, trying to flee Albania. Sinan was the only one who survived, protected from the blast by his mother's arms. Even he did not know this until a few years ago, when I told him in the heat of an argument, after my husband died. He said that he'd always felt that his life was not his own, that it had ended long ago. After this, Sinan and I became strangers, even on the occasions we spent some time together."

She watched some children throwing snowballs in front of the restaurant window.

"But he returned to Sarajevo," I said.

"To die." She waved at someone through the window. "And to get me out of Sarajevo. You see, he felt he owed me that much. So, the fact that it is you who sit here and not him, well, it's enough to say I am not surprised." She stood and kissed a man whose skin was as tanned as her own. I saw the Kid walking down the street, still flanked by both soldiers.

"Is that your son?" she asked, squeezing into her coat.

"It is Sinan's, rather."

She laughed, too loud.

"You cannot make a real grandmother out of a false mother. You are mixing your subjects, Jovan. Besides, how much sense does it make to try and save something which has been destroying you all along?"

She bent over me, shoved a bill in my pocket.

"I wish you a pleasant trip," she said. "If you know where it is you are going."

"I don't," I said.

"Then we will not be going to the same place," she said as she left.

❖ ❖ ❖

I am looking at what remains of the Don River. Were it not for the bridge, it would be hard to imagine that this creek had once been a river. Once upon a happy time, families probably walked across it just to show that they were families and that they were happy. Now plain clothes police patrol it, keeping suicides from their endings.

Huddled in the corner of the bed, the Kid shouts in his dream. There are the usual words: fire, bridge, river. Above his head there's an enlarged photo of myself and Sinan in a long line of people with containers waiting to fill them with water. Over Sinan's head the Kid has drawn an angel's halo. My face has been smeared by a red marker. Puerto Rican Ana will be here soon with the scent of December on her coat. A cab will come to fetch me.

I thought Sinan had died on the Sarajevo Bridge.

THE GAME

I WOULD NEVER HAVE MOVED into this big world if the air and smoke from my burning house hadn't forced me out of my small one, a small town in Bosnia inhabited by simple people, with simple wants and desires. Before the war started, the only smoke we had to contend with came from barbecues, or the cigarettes which stung our eyes the worst in the City Coffee Shop, where the *No Smoking* sign was posted. In the beginning, the owner of the coffee shop was very angry about our lack of respect for non-smokers. We in turn accused him of false advertising, since our town never did obtain city status. Later, he started smoking himself. The only gunpowder we ever came into contact with was at New Years, when we drunkenly played with fire crackers.

Then the war started, lasting so long I was forced to exchange this small, familiar world for that of a big Canadian city. This has now been reduced to a dark back yard, which I watch through the small window of my basement apartment.

This is not my window and this is not my apartment. Only my eyes are still my own.

My wide circle of friends has been reduced to self-serving neighbourhood cats, which drop by when I cook, and sparrows which wander about out of sheer boredom. I have now lived here for months, and everybody who passes says hello, though I never get to really know a single person. My neighbours pass and smile at me, but with no more warmth than that shown by the attendants on my flight to Toronto. In their smiles I see my own transience. There is nothing else. They are only interested in me because I have been standing at this same window now for months, watching the back yard. Sometimes I feel that I am transparent, and look behind me for my shadow. I've come from a world of Bosnian ruins, from a world slowly transforming itself into the world of black and white photographs and old newspaper clippings which fade as fast as my notes, written with a ballpoint pen on the page's margin. My friends, scattered around the world, have become strangers; I have followed after them to become a new resident of a new city, and a stranger to myself.

I watch sparrows fighting for chunks of bread so big and heavy they cannot take flight. They remind me of my friends and our Sunday soccer games. We played together for years. It was our sacred time. What Sunday mass is for the devoted.

Only death or an illness in the family was ever accepted as a valid excuse for non-attendance. At seven o'clock, exactly, we would put on our freshly laundered uniforms, player numbers at the back, our team sponsor *Healthy Living* on the front, thanks to the local pharmacy, the only sponsor we could find. Sundays became veggie days and we used only our childhood nicknames.

All seven of us had been raised on the same street and we were never far from one another. We'd done it all together, been through the wringer, from first loves to adolescent family fights. My father used to say we would have married each other. In some ways, never separated, we never had to grow up.

Where are they all now? In an old note-book in which I used to write the scores of our Sunday games I have recorded what I have been able to learn. I feel sick about it all when I think of it, when I open this note-book of our shared passion, because all I have left after I close it is melancholy, and the knowledge that we will never meet again.

Cabbage (Kupus). We called him this because of his curly, unruly hair which not even gallons of gel were able to tame. I have never seen such a fearless goalkeeper. He would throw himself at the feet of attacking players as if it were a matter of life and death. He would put his massive body in front of a ball flying with the speed of a projectile, and with the mastery of a wizard defend his goal. Rarely would he end a game without bruises. He had little use for higher education, taking over his father's watch business, and was the first among us to marry. Nobody was very happy when he married some city girl, an art student, who it was rumoured had more talent between her legs than in her head. All of us knew that Cabbage was continuously pulling his wife out from under her many lovers; also, that he loved her with a blind and wild loyalty. He would always forgive her.

When the war started, he put on the uniform of the Bosnian Army and went to the trenches to defend our team from the enemy. The next year his wife fled to enemy territory, and love-crazy, he discarded his military uniform and went in search of her. He wore his *Healthy Living* jersey. After wandering for a few days, Serbian soldiers captured and beat him. They might have shot him if he hadn't lied and said that he'd crossed to fight on the Serbian side. In fact, he was spared because his father was a Serb. For the next six months he shot at those with whom he'd previously shared trenches, and took great pains not to hit even one of them.

When he heard that his wife had been seen on the

Croatian side, he once again took off his uniform and joined the Croatian Army. He was once again beaten, and most likely would have been hung if his mother had not been Croatian. The next six months he spent in Croatian trenches shooting at the Serb and Bosnian armies.

After the war, Cabbage called just once to say that he was living in Zurich where he worked as a bouncer in a popular bar. He said that he was living happily with his wife and that they now had a son.

"Let me know when you get our old team together," he told me, "and let everybody know that I still have my jersey."

His mother later wrote to me that Cabbage had overdosed at least twice, that he almost died. Also, that his son is unusually dark.

Red Pepper (Paprika). There was no player in the world that ran as much during a game as Red Pepper. The only weakness he had was that he could not stand to lose, and when we lost a game he would insult us all. Then he would apologize for days. We always forgave Red Pepper, for all of us knew that from his seventh year he lived in an orphanage, and that he never stopped blaming himself for surviving the car accident that had killed his parents. Red Pepper was in charge of the Fire Station, and he was the first to organize the defence of our town when the war started. His fame grew so great that songs were written to celebrate his courage. The President of the country invited him to the capital, gave him a badge for courage and a job as his personal bodyguard. Quite possibly his fame would have spread and he would have been given a hero's medal if Red Pepper hadn't arrested the President's son, publicly accusing him of buying fuel of suspicious quality from the enemy. Even this scandal would've probably died down if Paprika had not called a press conference, accusing the President's son and blaming him for the deaths of five Sarajevan families burned alive while trying to warm themselves on stoves heated by the contaminated diesel.

No news stations reported Red Pepper's discovery. The songs about his courage disappeared from the radio.

A little later a bomb exploded in his car.

I helped him to his wheelchair when he left the hospital; I also helped him when they brought him to the bus station, so that he could leave the city. As the bus pulled away he slipped his badge into my hand and asked me to bury it behind the soccer field at seven o'clock sharp. I told him I didn't have the courage for it, but he didn't hear me. The last thing I saw was his soccer jersey, which he waved through the window of the bus.

I did get a letter from him. He wrote that he now lives in Australia and works at a public swimming pool. "Please let me know when you get the old team together so I can come and watch." But there was no return address on the envelope.

Cucumber (Krastavac). His shot was so powerful it left bruises on opposing players who got in its way, bruises which lasted until their next game. But Cucumber was very sensitive. When arguments with the other team broke out, mostly because of Pepper, he would withdraw to the other end of the field where he couldn't hear any swearing, and wait until the argument was over. At the end of the sixties he was the first and only hippy in our town. Since his father, a bank clerk, had been sentenced and jailed for embezzling, Cucumber lived alone with his mother in a tiny Bosnian house. He had a rather successful business making unique leather belts and bags.

Just when he had learned to live without his father, a few years before the war, his father was released from jail. Then the war started in his house. His father behaved as though fifteen years had not passed. And Cucumber, rather than listening to his father's lectures about how he needed to cut his hair and find respectable work, spent more and more time at the neighbourhood bar.

When his father sold the house to pay his lawyers to re-open the case that had led to his sentencing, both Cucumber and his mother found themselves on the street. In the end, his father again lost his case, and ended up in a nursing home, while Cucumber and his mother lived in the basement of a house that had once belonged to them. "I was born in the attic, lived my whole life on the first floor and I have ended up in the basement. I cannot go down any further," he once complained to me.

When the war started, Cucumber had already lost so much weight that the Military Command forbade him to voluntarily give blood. By sheer coincidence they sent him to evacuate the old people from the Nursing Home, who had endured for days without food or electricity. By another twist of fate, Cucumber entered his father's room, and his father promptly chased him out, ordering him to cut his hair and take his shoes off if he wanted to save him. "I slammed the door and left," he wrote to me in his last letter, just before he went crazy.

Someone told me that Cucumber is now the youngest resident of that Nursing Home, that he has cut his hair, but that he never takes off our *Healthy Living* team jersey.

Walnut. (Orah). The nickname came from his childhood, when he made a bet that he could smash his bedroom door with his head, thus proving that it was as hard as a walnut. He won the bet, though there is still a big scar on his head. But he could truly pass the ball with his head so precisely it was as if he were using his hand. He was also a brilliant dribbler. He was involved in all sorts of illegal activities, from scalping soccer tickets to selling counterfeit bus passes. He had a reputation as a great lover and we used to listen to his juicy stories for hours. He once claimed that he'd screwed seven of his father's eight wives. His father was the town's best doctor, and we never fully believed him until after his father died of a heart attack. Walnut continued to live with his stepmother. He told me that he did so because his vindictive father had left all of his estate to her. The only thing he left Walnut in the will was his real mother's diary. His mother had been a famous Sarajevan beauty who had hanged herself before she'd even breast fed the newborn Orah. Nobody knew what was in the diary except Orah, and he, who talked about everything else, never said a word about it. Only once did he mention that his mother predicted his future before she died.

Thanks to his father's friends, he acquired a white hospital gown, and in this way he hid himself from military duty by assisting in the Hospital crematorium.

"Please do not talk about this to anyone," he wrote to me. "Today I have cremated my mother for the last time. They have brought her here from the mortuary seven times. I hope that this is the last time, and that the only thing left for me to do is burn her diary." After that I did not hear about him for months until his stepmother wrote to me, asking me to find out the address of the bastard Walnut, who talked her into selling the house by promising plane tickets to Hawaii and a happy life together. "After he ran away with all the money, I felt so dead," she wrote me, and offered me his soccer jersey in exchange for his address.

"Don't even think about it," Walnut wrote to me on the back of his funeral home brochure. "In any case, I have too many corpses in my life."

It appeared that his business was doing well.

Where does he live? I will never tell.

Carrot (Mrkva). His height of two metres enabled him to win every challenge for a ball in the air. We used to talk for days about his clever and unusual goals. I've never known anyone else who could remember such a huge collection of jokes, or spend days dreaming up cheerful gags. He believed that human beings were such funny creatures that the continuation of the human race depended upon how much we could laugh at ourselves. Once he called the police, an anonymous tip, and claimed that our opponents were hiding drugs in their running shoes. Both teams started the game with only socks on their feet. He did not think it too much trouble to drill a hole behind a mailbox and wait for days just to catch the postman's hand while he was delivering the mail. He thought it terribly funny that he was the only citizen the postman refused to deliver mail to.

Since high school, Carrot had always won the state shooting contests. The Bosnian Army recruited him as a sniper at the beginning of the war, and deployed him to one of the Sarajevan apartment buildings to shoot at the Serbian side. They told him not to spare any bullets and he listened. He also told me that he'd never had as much fun as he had then, shooting at soldiers' heels, their glasses of cognac or lit cigarettes. Then a sniper bullet from the other side hit his younger brother in the head, and Carrot's famous smile disappeared. The next time I saw him, people were already calling him the "Sarajevo Monster" because his favourite target had become children on their way home from school. And every time he would get a child on the other side of the river, some sniper who was also called "the Sarajevo Monster" would get a child on the Bosnian side. That Serbian sniper, and Carrot, had already created whole cemeteries of little graves.

The killing game would have continued for who knows how long if a foreign journalist had not found out about the strangely similar statistics of dead children on both sides.

Ironically, they took the rifle away from Carrot and made him an elementary school principal in town. Perhaps everybody would have forgotten Carrot the sniper, the monster, perhaps he would have regained his reputation as a great joker, if only his eye had not one day grown so big with disease that it covered almost half of his face.

I found him one day at my door, wearing our team jersey. I couldn't even look at him. "I'm going now to the other side to see if anybody there looks like me" he said. "Don't write down the score. This is my private game."

I never found out the score. Carrot simply disappeared, in the way new jobs appear and disappear. I still keep the notebook in which he used to write down the world's best jokes. But I tell them to no one.

Raspberry (Malina). Together with Carrot he brought real chaos to the defense, and if the two had not so often competed with one another for goals, I doubt that we would have ever lost even a single game. What brilliant technique by this tall, skinny, and always troubled player. He never truly laughed, and all of us somehow avoided making jokes on his account. After his father's accidental death, when he was buried in a mine, Raspberry was adopted by Carrot's parents—prosperous engineers who worked for the same mining company. He'd never known his mother. He was raised together with Carrot and they became so close that all the locals thought of them as twins.

This lasted until Carrot's brother was born. Then Raspberry became quiet and withdrawn. He was moved into the maid's room in order to prepare his old one for the newborn.

After that, the house met with disasters that nobody could explain. First, Carrot's mother, who was pregnant again, disappeared on the way to the hospital. She was later found, dead. Carrot's father was taking a wreath made of fresh flowers to the cemetery when he disappeared as well. The florist, who had made the wreath, swore to me that for nights he saw it going back and forth, from their house to the cemetery, night after night. But who was going to believe an envious florist whose wife was working as a maid in Carrot's house? After the funeral, Raspberry moved out, and for a long time worked as an ordinary miner, before being promoted to the position of Head Engineer. We would only see him at our Sunday games and other occasional sporting events.

He always won second prize in shooting competitions. Carrot, the champion, always came back to Sarajevo with the first prize money and we celebrated his victories in the City Coffee Shop. Raspberry always returned with him, carrying a new gun as consolation prize. We knew the number of

Raspberry's rifles just by counting Carrot's winning medals.

At the beginning of the war, Raspberry disappeared together with his collection of rifles and the florist's wife. I found under my door on the day he left a note asking me to erase his name from my note-book because he was going on a mission that he could not disclose anything about. He did not leave his jersey behind.

There were rumours, after his disappearance, that he had been seen in a Serbian uniform. But I don't know anything about this. I can only speculate.

Lemon (Limun). I am he. It is in the nature of games for someone to play and someone else to watch. Only occasionally would I be put in goal for a few minutes, usually when Cabbage would go to the phone to check on his wife. My left leg has always been shorter than my right, so my job was to write down the scores of our games and to take care of the water. If it wasn't for my note-book, all those passionate Sunday games would have been forgotten as though they had never taken place.

Waiting in a long passport control line at the Toronto airport, a woman asked me if I had a need to forget the sorrow of the war. "God forbid," I told her, "I am ashamed that I've already started forgetting."

I cannot remember anybody from the other teams. I am unable to recall their faces, though I can still see them as if through a haze, exhausted and angry after losing yet another game. I can still smell the sweat in their jerseys. I can still hear the swearing while they put their running shoes, wet towels, and sweaty shirts into their bags. Next Sunday, they consoled themselves, we will return and take our revenge on *Healthy*

Living for this shameful defeat. I can still see them leaving the dressing rooms, until the only things that remain are their shadows in the distance.

There was a goalie, skinny and pale as death, who had called us the *Snow Men*, and prophesized that sooner or later we would all melt, leaving behind our jerseys in puddles. Even this goalie I can only see through a fog.

Most likely, he doesn't even remember me that well. I know the effort it would take to picture the crippled guy warming the bench, the one always writing something down in his note-book, and who for all those years never forgot to call the players and remind them of the Sunday games at seven.

He is probably even now sitting beside some window in a city whose name will take time to remember, watching sparrows fight for crumbs too big to fly with.

"It must have been terrible to live through the war," the woman said. "It will be a relief to live now in peace after all those years of war."

She looked at my shabby jersey, rifled through with holes, stained by sweat.

"Do you think I will be able to get used to peace," I asked her. Then I gave my note-book to the customs official, who had just asked if I had any valuables.

SATURDAY

"YOU'RE GETTING OLD, my darling. You resemble a deflated balloon. You don't even want to hide it. When you get up in the morning, there's more hair left on your comb than you've got on your head. I can see it better than you can."

"You don't see anything, Maria," Josip thinks, not without the queasiness that he has always felt upon hearing her sharp voice. He says nothing. He only leans further through the open window, tries to drown her out in the racket from the street. "If some day I fall out of this window," he thinks, "it won't be by accident."

"You're also becoming forgetful. I can't tell any more whether I can send you to the store. Do you know what the fat lady on cash register five asked me this morning? The one with three kilos of make-up on her face? 'How old is your brother?' 'Pardon!' Her smile disgusts me. 'He's not my brother, he's my husband,' I tell her, though you really do look older than I do. 'Really,' she says, 'somehow you look more like brother and sister.' 'Oh really,' I go, 'what makes you think so?'"

"Nothing in particular," Josip replies to himself. It's the third time he's heard this story. It happened two days ago. She even called the store manager to complain.

"'Nothing in particular,' she says. Who knows what she meant? Did you forget to pay again? On the other hand, I suppose it's not unusual for you to feel so unwell in your old age."

"I'm not that old. I'm 64, and I don't feel unwell at all," Josip mumbles. He bends further out the open window. Even after years of shopping in the same grocery store she still doesn't know the cashier's name. Teresa, her name is Teresa, he calls out to her, though only in his mind.

The neon balls over *Robert's Bar* flash every second, lending a distinctive, even festive, beauty to the faces of passers-by. Some turn into the bar. For some, it is a matter of habit. Others make the turn because it is Saturday and they need to do something different. Josip can almost hear them. Those at the bar will discuss the Jays' latest loss, lamenting that the players get far more money than they're worth. "If they'd only give me back all the money I've wasted on tickets so far," somebody will observe, "I'd be a god."

Pissing in the washroom, the gossip will be about Greek Julia—who for months has been squandering the inheritance she received from her father—waiting until closing time to pick up someone who doesn't have a better idea about how to spend a Saturday. Or someone drunk enough not to notice that she's so fat that she has to sit on two chairs. Everybody respects her so long as she's sober, since nobody else can explain so clearly why the Blue Jays lose over and over.

"They lose to give us a reason to drink." It is her clinching argument. Then, she orders double whiskeys for everyone who likes her joke. Poor Julia.

A few nights ago, drunk as usual, her neighbours heard her howling as Ron closed the bar. "Christ, where did you hide my man?" A drunken male voice was heard to respond. "This is Christ speaking, Julia. Fuck off."

The older ones, not up for a morning hangover, will stay

away from the bar and play pool. The younger ones will chat over tepid beer and try not to attract too much attention when they go to the washroom to smoke a joint. Kajubi's going around with his head bandaged, after he threw himself through the window of Chang-Loo's restaurant out of sheer happiness when he saw on TV that his lottery number had been drawn. For a long time after that he was ashamed to show his face on the street because he'd forgotten to bet his usual ticket. Besides, the bill for the broken glass awaited him.

Around midnight, Brian will come in to dilute his loss with bitter whiskey, something he's done almost nightly since his son bet his drunken friends that he could swim across Lake Ontario. Those who emerge from the bar at midnight will have the same expressions on their faces as they had when they went in.

"Why do you keep interrupting me? That Balkan urge of yours not to let people finish a sentence drives me crazy. A man your age should have more respect for others. . . . now look what you've done! I forget what I wanted to tell you."

"You wanted to tell me I'm getting old," Josip reminds her, blinking, a sudden cool breeze on his face. When God creates the world next time he should be more considerate and shorten the summer by at least half. And add it to the Spring.

Mimi's standing at the corner near *Robert's Bar* again, waiting for someone willing to pay not to be alone part of the night. She's now under the protection of the Spaniard Bastos, the one who disfigured Paolo's face with a razor hidden between two fingers for being called a nigger. No one believed that he'd show up in the street after he got out of jail. But here he is, selling Mimi and brushing invisible hairs off of his jacket every time she touches him. Poor Mimi, head over heels in love again. This time maybe God will remind her that her last pimp took her savings and disappeared.

In the heat of the evening, old Eusebio sits in his dark booth at the entrance to the parking lot, probably sipping from his thermos the coffee brewed by his new wife. Thirty years younger, she looks after him as if he is her father. He doesn't seem to mind her boyfriends, or occasionally waiting for dawn before he can get into bed with her.

For the last two weeks, Harris' youngest son comes early to *Robert's Bar,* and always leaves late. A boy with a golden voice, he set out on a West Coast concert tour last year, with a lot of noise and pride. He returned recently, without his guitar, and with no money. Robert should be smart enough to offer him a contract, at least over the weekend.

Robert's Bar . . . Robert's Bar . . . Josip reads the neon sign a few more times to see if it makes him as sick as hearing Robert's name. Why this masochism, he asks himself, after a cramp darts through his stomach.

"Of course you're getting old, there's no doubt about it." Maria is still weaving her dissatisfaction, looking over her glasses at the expiry date on the butter container. "There's something else I want to tell you. God, what did I want to tell you? I forget because you keep interrupting. You always mumble and interrupt me. Oh, yes! I remember now. You didn't tell me anything about seeing Ana. As if you didn't go to Montreal at all. You just sit there and stare at *Robert's Bar.* You don't care if her mother doesn't know what she's doing."

"For God's sake, Maria," he says, trying to make his baritone more soft, "I've told you everything a hundred times already! But okay, once more: she's got a fairly good job at college and lives with a handsome Bosnian who fled the war. When he learns the language he'll get a job right away. There are always jobs for computer people. They love and look after each other. What else? They don't throw money away. They have enough."

Maria doesn't take her eyes off the butter container. His words don't seem to have any effect. That's all to the good, Josip tells himself and turns his attention once more to the street.

He spots the small round-shouldered figure of Shang in front of the bar, studying the menu in the window. Over the past couple of years, his restaurant, *Little China*, only gets the customers who know it is open all night. In February, he drew a kitchen knife on a merry-maker who jokingly ordered a hamburger and fries. His son lives with a young Brazilian immigrant and has been lying to him, for years, that he's a student of acupuncture. His wife and daughter moved to Hong Kong, allegedly to open a restaurant, but rumour has it that they've only a shop window in the red-light district.

He will stand in front of the price list for a long time, holding the hand of Philip, the gym teacher, dubbed "Filipino girl" by the high school kids.

"What do you mean *enough*?" Maria's quarrelsome voice draws Josip back in. "That means nothing to me. It never occurs to you to give me details. Like, where they go shopping, whether they plan to have kids. You spent three days at their place and I get three seconds out of it. You could have said more in a telegram. What language do they talk in?"

"They speak our language. . . ."

"Which 'our language'?"

A language in which you and I cannot understand one another, he wants to tell her, but instead of this he hears himself saying: "Okay. They're talking in a language we used to speak better than the one we speak now. And, by the way, I don't intend to argue with you about language again. They live like the rest of the normal world. They love each other. It's enough for me."

He says this as if closing the door after a pesky guest. Her thin black figure does not move. She still studies the date on the butter dish. It is as if she has not heard him.

Will this farce ever end? he wonders. I didn't have to go to Montreal. It should have been her. Ana's not my daughter, she's Maria's. She didn't want to go but sent me instead, so that she could suck my blood for days. I must be the last fool on earth who believes her migraines don't let her travel.

Perhaps she'd rather hear that nobody was waiting for me at the station in Montreal; that I almost didn't find their damp, filthy basement apartment. That I was disgusted with their bed linen. That I was afraid of the big grey rat that came out of the wall and drank the water out of the glass where I put my dentures. Maybe she'd like better than me the wonderful son-in-law who can't close the bathroom door when, in the middle of talking, he goes in to shoot a new dose of morphine. Or that her daughter works at the college as a cleaner and rummages my pockets for change when she comes home. She should have heard Ana shout at me when I offered to pay her ticket back to Toronto, with me.

"You're crazy if you think that I could spend a day in the same apartment with that woman."

It would be simpler if she asked why I stayed only three days when I had planned to stay seven, or why I went to a hotel the second day. If she had been the one to go, it would have been easier for me to pretend that I didn't notice her going to the post office and sending Ana money. Then she could show some gratitude from time to time for knowing how to keep quiet and my eyes shut.

In a skirt that hardly covers her underpants, swaying her hips, Carrie passes by *Robert's Bar*. It does not suffice to say that she carries fire inside. Better to say flames. She doesn't miss the chance to look at herself in the window, and gives the finger to two sweaty guys inside the bar who give her the same. She's been looking for her husband Paul, with a knife in her hand, since he told her last Christmas that the sperm he'd been endlessly pouring into her for years had finally achieved something worth mentioning with a young Romanian girl. The rumour is that Paul fled to Romania and that he has a whole bunch of kids. Now she's not giving him a divorce until she finds a new husband.

Perhaps there's some truth in that stupid waiter Stan's story that Carrie once took him to her apartment just after the bar closed, arousing him so much that he agreed to dress up in Paul's wedding suit and make love to her. It is easier to believe the story than to imagine that Stan made it up.

It's been days since anyone has seen Halim, the fruit and vegetable man, an inveterate bachelor who carries just enough change to pay for a beer. Not a penny more. Once, when he got drunk on the tab of three guys from the fish store, he revealed his grasp of mathematics: it doesn't pay to marry; it is cheaper to use Mimi's services once a month. Once, he almost choked to death from asthma in front of the bar. Asthma medication costs too much.

"And that's all you have to tell me? You can't remember

anything else? I could hear more from someone driving through Montreal than I can from you."

❖ ❖ ❖

It is Saturday. On Saturdays Maria's nerves stretch to snapping. Always on Saturdays, when the city starts to resemble a city, and when Josip has an enormous urge to be different. But Maria doesn't like theatres because they're crass and because actresses look like prostitutes. Maria runs to her room when Josip turns on the TV because Satan invented television in order to make us stupid. Maria does not even like answering the phone. Saturday is the ugly day before Sunday.

"How do you want your eggs?"

"Two eggs easy over and a sausage between them," Josip answers mechanically, leaning low towards the street so that he can better see the figure of Gaetano's new wife. He pretends not to hear Maria's opinion that he is being salacious.

Gaetano is really an incurable old lecher, he thinks, not without some jealousy. Flowers haven't wilted on his last wife's grave, and he's already off to the bar with a new one. She's looking at him happily over her surgically lifted, voluminous breasts. She must be at least twenty years Gaetan's junior, perhaps more. She tenderly passes her fingers through what's left of his hair and lets him open the door of *Robert's Bar* for her. Josip tries to remember whether this is Gaetano's sixth or seventh marriage, and how many of his wives have ended up in the cemetery. Like the late Lilian, an Irish girl and Robert's former waitress. Guys from the fish market used to leave their entire weekly pay cheque just go get a look at her incredibly large breasts. When Gaetano opened an antique store on the street fifteen years ago everybody thought it was suicide. Today he lives off of the interest on the money he lends. If Josip leaned through the window just a tiny bit more, he might just hear Gaetano's famous order: "Drinks for everybody in *Robert's Bar*, including the rats in the cemetery," just before the door closes behind the huge butt of his new wife.

Robert's Bar . . . Robert's Bar . . . Josip tracks the length of the neon sign, trying to pronounce the words normally, as his mouth would shape the words on the parking lot sign over the dark booth Eusebio sits in, pondering. But the words press on his stomach like rocks. It would be easier to pronounce "Josip's Bar," he thinks, though he feels no better for it.

"You really are a joker." He hears her quarrelsome voice from the kitchen. It would have been better if he'd said he wasn't hungry. From the corner of his eye he sees her tiny black figure by the stove. He also sees her cross herself.

"Two eggs and a sausage. I imagine that up there in the Bosnian hills you grew up with only one thought in your head: get a hold of a wife." She speaks without taking a breath. "But I can't believe that forty years hasn't been enough to think of something better. As if you never got out to that stinking bar. Why don't you look at me when we're talking? Why are you looking through that window? What do you see in that disgusting street?"

He misses the moment when Mimi disappears from the street. Who did she go with? Josip watches Bastos pick invisible hairs off of his sleeve.

"I see what you can't," he answers flatly, knowing that if he says more Maria will start to cry.

Maria hates Saturday. "Saturday is the day devils adopted," Maria says, staring angrily at the T-shirt Josip puts on every Saturday before he sits, opens the window, and watches the street. The T-shirt has faded so much from washing that the sign "Robert's Bar" seems hardly there. "I hope it disintegrates before you do," Maria sometimes says, and Josip smiles, slyly, because he has duplicates of the same T-shirt Maria doesn't know about. Maria responds to her husband's smile with her own, and the secret that she's discovered yet another under the washer. Josip smiles more broadly, because he was smart enough to hide the T-shirts in two different places.

She's no longer the dark angel who appeared to Josip six years ago.

Long ago, on a hung-over Saturday afternoon, while cleaning a floor covered with torn lottery tickets, he forgot to put up the *closed* sign on the door. Maria came in, with a girl almost as tall as she was, arguing about a ring that had disappeared from the girl's finger. The girl answered in English, and did not hide her boredom, but Maria spoke in a language whose every word smelled of Josip's ancestral homeland—the abandoned family home, the grass around the house, the fresh air; the Bosnia he remembered from childhood.

While he stealthily watched her in the mirror over the bar, Maria told the girl that she wouldn't tolerate her absences from school, and he couldn't suppress a sudden silly smile.

"What's funny, sir?" Maria asked him when he put coffees on their table.

"Nothing in particular," Josip answered, in Bosnian. In the language he had almost forgotten.

"Instead of eavesdropping, you could wash your cups better," Maria said.

"Really?" Josip asked. "Do you think that you could do better?"

"It's the least thing that should be washed in here. Maybe the best thing would be to put the whole bar in the washer."

"Well, if that's the case, you've got the job."

"I wasn't looking for a job," she said, "but since Mr. Josip, it's you making the offer, I accept."

"How do you know my name?" he asked, a bit confused.

"It says so on your T-shirt," Maria told him, casting a reproachful glance at her daughter, who giggled at Josip's blushing face.

When she returned that evening, she brought some order to the glasses and cups. The next day the bar was so clean and polished that you could have mistaken it for a mirror. The long-forgotten manufacturer's colour returned to the fridges, and Josip pretended not to hear the old regulars grunting that the beer smelled more and more of disinfectant and less and less of beer.

He watched her and marvelled at the ease with which she found work. She would go to the far end of the city to make dinner for her daughter, then to the church kitchen to serve dinner to the homeless, before returning in the evening to pick up where she'd left off. He was pleased with the order this tiny, solemn woman made. He'd never seen her laugh. Even when she smiled, it looked like a faded memory, or a painful grimace. Even chatty Julia, who could make a dead man speak, gave up on Maria.

"She can't speak English, or she's deaf and dumb," she said and left her alone.

Maria's presence brought sadness to the bar, a sadness that everybody was a bit ashamed of. Especially after TV newscasts showed the horror of the Bosnian war.

"You know how I hate it when you talk to me and watch me in the mirror," Maria says, polishing a pan that sparkles already. "And I don't like it when you watch my back in the bottom of the pan," he wants to reply, but a tenor voice reaches him from *Robert's Bar,* singing a sorrowful Irish song.

My God, he thinks, it can only be Ron. I can't believe he's back. There were few people Josip loved as much as he loved the dutiful student Ron. He'd once called him his son. The twiggy youth would sit at a table in a corner of the bar all evening, studying for university exams and drinking one coffee after another. He was probably the only Irishman Josip had met who toasted with a cup of coffee. Had he not taken breaks by climbing every half hour on the table and singing an Irish ballad, Irishmen would probably have scorned him. Josip melted at the sound of his voice and secretly paid him five dollars for each song. This was Josip's contribution to his studies.

But perhaps it isn't Ron's voice after all.

Maria hadn't liked him. Whenever he started singing, she'd turn on the TV. Ron bore this until, one night, finally unnerved, he'd picked up his thick books and left, swearing that he would never return as long as the black-dressed woman worked there. He was smart enough not to force Josip to choose between Irish songs and Bosnian sorrow, since everybody had already noticed that Josip no longer missed his morning shave, and that he was finally wearing ironed shirts.

And it suddenly seemed to Josip that life had more meaning

than closing at midnight and reopening while it was still morning, that there might be more for him than calling cabs for guests who had forgotten their addresses. And, yes, drunken hockey fans who loved to take it out on the owner when the Maple Leafs lost. He might even live without the stray hookers who would leave their sweaty beds, taking everything that they could get hold of. He'd always felt that a different order could be brought to his life, a thought that had never left him. It did him good to resurrect the language of his homeland, with a tiny woman washing glasses at the bar, next to him, even if he couldn't read anything but sorrow on her face.

He didn't complain too much when she turned his small office behind the bar—where he used to often spend the night—into a used clothes depot. Nor when she filled the bar with canned donations for the Bosnian refugees who were arriving, thin as shadows.

Though he did not like how she arranged the tables in the bar, he hadn't said a word. Dirty stories that used to be the bar's trademark began after ten, after Maria had gone home. He pretended not to notice how old customers asked with their eyes how long they'd have to put up with the storm that swept their glasses away before they finished their drinks. He did notice when they stopped coming. Even the old baker, Ferdo, who'd sat on the same bar stool at nine o'clock sharp for ten years, and who claimed that Death, if she wanted to show some consideration, would have to wait for him in front of *Josip's Bar*. "There are only three things in life you can't hide: love, stupidity, and poverty," he told Josip. "Soon, I'm afraid you won't even be able to hide the third." Then he left Josip's bar forever. It happened only a week or so after Maria finished painting the washrooms black.

Maria had moved into his life in the form of clean bed sheets and ironed shirts, in the form of cooked dinners and endless stories of a once-beautiful homeland now inhabited by a million buried land mines. For hours, they'd sit in the empty bar and talk, searching for the forgotten words of yore, now tarnished by English, searching for the juice of meaning lost a long time ago. Her hands were so soft when she talked about the beauty of the Bosnian countryside; her shoulders had the fragrance of wild Bosnian forests. But her eyes never smiled when their chats came to an end. Yes, we'll go back to Bosnia soon, she'd say, but her face would change into a grimace of pain and he noticed how sorrow cut her dream to pieces. After that she'd speak to him the way she'd talk to a ghost of the past. Yes, we're going back to Bosnia but promise me you'll never drink on Saturday. Promise me you'll never touch me the way man touches woman on Saturday, because man needs to hurt people that day.

"What happened to you, Maria, in that camp?" He'd try to break down the invisible wall of horror, but after he asked, Maria would walk behind the counter and wash already-clean glasses and he'd sit alone with her shadow, noting how the beer he was drinking tasted bitter.

"Sit down Maria and talk to me."

"No, Josip, no. Talk to your glass of beer."

❖ ❖ ❖

"Why are you gawking at that bar? One day you'll fall out of that window. Don't tell me you miss that stinking den and all those alcoholics and bums. A man your age should think more and daydream less." Her voice rattles like the pots above her head.

"You didn't even open the letter you got from the Funeral Home. If you had, you'd have noticed that you're paying only my monthly installments. They're asking what about your payments. If you keep from opening that letter, some new young employee may not believe you're forgetful."

"I'm not ready to die yet, but when I decide to die I'll die in my homeland," Josip replies. He concentrates on Mimi, now back on the street, removing invisible hairs from her lips. A blowjob is cheaper, but also quicker.

"Nonsense, you won't die in the homeland unless you live there," Maria says.

"Well, then, I wonder what we're doing here," Josip replies, tracking Bastos, who is trying to avoid Mimi's kiss, his focused fingers deftly counting her money. Then Bastos suddenly starts shouting. He grabs Mimi by her hair and slaps her so hard that she staggers and falls among the garbage bags. She gets up and starts screaming so loudly that the song from the bar abruptly stops. Robert appears at the door with two other men. Bastos takes a knife out of his pocket and waves it at them. At that moment, police sirens suddenly howl and three cars, their lights on, dash into the parking lot. Surprised, Bastos flings aside his knife, drops the white jacket over his arm, and runs down the street. Robert and a skinny guy holding his pants up with one hand chase after him. Another man helps Mimi, who has stopped screaming, get up. My God, Josip thinks, he resembles Ron so much. Only he's fatter and balder.

The cops, who had jumped out of their car as if about to

dismantle time, merely cast an offhand glance at the three running men, as if looking at fools who had nothing better to do than jog on Saturday night. They go straight to Eusebio's booth in the parking lot. A few flash bulbs go off. A woman with a camera on her shoulder tries to thrust her microphone over the cops' shoulders when they come out of the booth, leading a handcuffed Eusebio. Holding a cup of coffee in one hand, he smiles, as if he's just been to a good show. Poor Eusebio. It seems that he really has no luck with women. Or maybe women have no luck with him.

"That is my homeland over there," Josip mumbles, looking towards the bar.

All of Robert's customers are out on the sidewalk to see what is going on. Mimi peeps through the bar window, holding a cloth to her face with one hand, and with the other taking invisible hairs off Bastos's jacket, which she is now wearing.

"If you think you could have got more for that dump of a bar, you're very mistaken. If it hadn't been for Robert, it would still be for sale."

Maria's black dressing gown is shouting, on the verge of tears already.

Blue and red from the police lights reflect off the surfaces of the pots in the kitchen.

❖ ❖ ❖

"I have nothing to give you," she told him that Saturday when Josip proposed to her. For the first time she admitted she had been in a prisoners' camp with her daughter. "I've experienced horror you cannot dream of. Don't ask me about it because I stopped living then. I do not need somebody to start a new life with. What I need is somebody I can die with." She said it in a single breath. Josip froze. At that moment, he could see the Maria who screamed in her dreams, the Maria who hid the deep knife scars on her back left by a camp guard, the Maria whose past had died and whose future resembled her past more and more. It was not the Maria who would want children. It was not the Maria whose hair smelled like the grass in front of Josip's old family house, beautiful and soft. But it was the only Maria left to him. Where was that army of Saturday night friends who had promised to stay friends no matter what? They are sitting and drinking in *Robert's Bar*, having trouble remembering the name of the guy who used to run *Robert's Bar*.

On the day he'd made his great decision there was nobody to celebrate it with. Only Mimi showed up, asking for change for a fifty dollar bill, unable to finish her cognac because a stranger was waiting for the rest of the money outside the bar. At his wedding, there was no one he could call a friend. Just Mimi again, who spent more time asking the young minister for a loan than paying attention to the service. Not to mention a few old drunks, who Maria chased out when they started making jokes about the honeymoon night. There was Robert, who acted as Maria's best man. Ah, fucking Robert. And her daughter Ana, who couldn't contain her laughter when he said yes.

Was it making love, those times in the dark of Josip's former office, surrounded by the bags of used clothes the Bosnian refugees no longer picked up? Making something, perhaps, but certainly not love. Maria screamed in pain every time Josip touched her. No, Maria, no. I'm not a soldier. My body isn't a camp. I'm just a lonely man who doesn't want to feel his hand rejected because it looks like somebody else's. I'm not a soldier: my skin is the only uniform I'll ever wear. No, Maria, I'm not going to rape you, and I'm not going to add another scar to your back. Sleep well, Maria, and don't forget we're still alive. Yes, I promise I'll never again read out loud newspaper reports about rape in prisoners' camps. It's just that sometimes, I feel lonely spending most of my time with your ghosts.

"It looks like we're having a hot Saturday night," he calls to Maria over his shoulder. But Maria isn't in the kitchen any longer. Her usual Saturday migraines. His eyes are glued to the street.

A bunch of people stand in front of *Robert's Bar* with beers in their hands, watching the police cars leave the parking lot. Everybody is talking at once. No matter how much Josip leans over, he can't understand a word. With his bandaged head, Kajubi ardently explains something to an indifferent Brian, who in turn staggers, a glass of whiskey in his hand. Next to them, fat Julia flails her arms, not caring about the beer spilling out of her glass, explaining something to round-shouldered Chang, who doesn't let go of Philip's hand. Halim tries to push his way closer to Julia, who always has a theory. He seems to be more attracted to Julia's theory than to Gaetano's, who also seems to be explaining something. His new wife stands on the side, nervously waving her fan and looking over the head of a mustachioed boy talking to her, his eyes glued to her huge breasts. The whole street shouting.

They are interrupted for a moment by a siren, then the ambulance dashing along the street. The shouting gets louder, carrying a few words on the wind. Julia's likely, as she is the loudest.

Soon afterwards, the guy who had chased Bastos with Robert appears at the end of the street. He still holds his pants up with one hand. A big bloody patch spreads in the middle of his T-shirt. Robert isn't with him.

When they see him, everybody falls silent. Gaetano's big-breasted wife screams, muffled by her fan. The skinny guy can't catch his breath as they surround him. Mimi runs out of the bar, screaming. The skinny guy is saying something to those who tighten their circle around him.

"What happened . . . what happened?" Josip shouts, leaning even further out the window. "Are you listening to me . . . I have to know."

Josip feels his feet lift, his toes no longer touching the floor. He yells shortly, topples from the window. He feels the heat of the asphalt as it rises to meet him. Somewhere high above, the voice of Maria, fading.

"I told you not to be so curious. Come back! Come back!"

Josip momentarily opens his eyes to the face of Ferdo, the baker, wavering above him. The crowd behind him is a blur.

"It's nice," he says, "to die in the homeland."

The last thing he hears is someone cursing, though he doesn't recognize the voice.

"Fuck Saturdays like this."

THE LEGEND OF ADAM THE FRAME

MR. GRIEG WAS EXHAUSTED when the last applicant for the position of Master Framer showed up. For the eighteenth time that day, he took out of the drawer a painting not bigger than a book depicting a tree trunk fighting the waves of a surging river, and for the eighteenth time that day he asked the same question: "How, dear sir, would you frame this painting?"

The man sitting across from him was bald, tall, unusually thin. He smiled briefly. "This painting," he said, "could not accept a frame. No frame would ever be strong enough to hold back the force of those waves."

A poet, Mr. Grieg thought, is the last thing I need today. Still, he had to admit that this guy was better than the previous applicant, who had believed Tom Thomson's painting a worthless modernist daub.

"And if I still insist on framing it?" Mr. Grieg asked, watching the beanpole's fingers hover over the picture.

"Then you do not need me," the beanpole said. He bowed slightly, and left the office.

Mr. Grieg watched him go. You're nothing special, he thought. He wished he'd told him that, then started, grabbed his key and jumped up. The workmen finishing the staircase watched as Mr. Grieg, the Director of the new Art Gallery of Ontario—soon to open—jumped over pails of paint and cement and ran after the thin man.

He's either a lunatic or a genius, Mr. Grieg thought. He

caught up with him, and pulled the thin man into the tiny room that only he had the key to. It was the hidden gallery of his worries and sleepless nights.

"Since you consider yourself a special master, solve this problem. If you do," he said, "you've got yourself a job." He showed the thin man the painting, *Fishing Boats at Sea*, by the old master Hendrik Willem Mesdag.

There seemed nothing out of the ordinary: fishing boats on a calm sea. But water oozed from the painting, making a pool on the floor. The thin man bent over and licked the water and without a trace of surprise explained that it was sea water and that he knew exactly what was needed.

"Only a frame made of ship-building wood can withstand the sea," he said. He promised that he would make the frame in a week. "I will," he said, "persuade the painting to move into it."

A week later, the workmen taking down the scaffold and packing away their brushes thought that Mr. Grieg had landed a huge inheritance. He seemed that happy. The thin man moved into the basement workshop, bringing with him only a bag of tools.

His name was Adam. He never told anyone his last name, so they called him Adam the Frame. No one knew where he'd come from, though his accent sounded European. Some believed that he must have come from the Belgian city of Antwerp, where the art of picture framing was so common that even children learned to make frames for the wonderful dreams they had.

When questioned, he said little. "I was born long ago and I come from nowhere." People assumed that he was over sixty although there were those who, studying Adam's pale unwrinkled face, believed he must be a spirit. Only a spirit could have resolved the Salon's many problems after the AGO opened.

Indeed, the Salon, the most beautiful room in the whole Gallery, reeked so badly of decay that everybody kept clear of it. Nothing helped: neither coats of paint on the wall, nor scents secretly placed in the room's nooks. Adam spent a whole night in the room and in the morning announced, coughing, that the stench derived from *Nature Morte aux Huitres*, by Gustave Caillebotte. The frame, he claimed, was too thin. He made a thick decorative frame and lowered the gallery's temperature to zero. The stench disappeared.

The trouble was, numerous visitors stood freezing in front of the painting. Someone remarked that the Gallery could make a lot of money selling hot tea. Somebody else spitefully wrote in the visitors' book that it was better to live in stench than to freeze to death.

Mr. Grieg did not refuse Adam's requests to occasionally spend a night alone with the paintings. The night watchman, Jovan the Bosnian, swore that he'd heard Adam talk a few times to the paintings in different languages, and that figures from paintings occasionally argued with him. One morning, frantic with fear, he reported to Mr. Grieg that a rainstorm had raged in Pavilion Two all night. But when they arrived, everything was fine, though they found Adam's pipe under Joseph Wright of Derby's *Antigonus in the Storm*.

Once, the painting, *The Fire in the Saint-Jean Quarter*, by Joseph Légaré, sent up smoke and smelled of burning for days and they had to put a barrel of water next to it in case the flames spread outside the frame. Adam put it into a new frame carved from northern woods and the painting calmed down. On another occasion, he placed the portrait of the pale Marchesa Casati in the sun for the day and colour, incredibly, returned to her face. He brought in a cat from the street and left it to spend the whole day among a series of cat paintings. Mr. Grieg joked that he was lucky not to have any elephant paintings in the Gallery.

The mystical way in which Adam reconciled a painting with its frame, or the painting with the Gallery wall, reconciled Adam with Mr. Grieg, who got used to being forbidden to enter the workshop while the master was working. Though he could do nothing about how sad Adam looked after his son Sebastian moved in.

Sebastian had just completed art studies in Paris and was both full of his own importance and scornful of others. He was the very opposite of his modest father. It was generally assumed that he'd mainly studied wines in Paris pubs, and that he'd spent more time in front of the mirror adjusting his black fedora than at his easel. He woke in the afternoon, then roamed the city with an empty sketchbook under his arm, ending the day in a restaurant where Adam used to eat. He always left his large bills for his father to pay. He professed that he painted by night and when Adam told him that his loud snoring didn't sound like work, he said that in his dreams he'd conceived of his first exhibition that would, beyond any doubt, be revolutionary and a world success. He showed his father some of his oil paintings. Caught between paternal love for his only son and the desire to rebuke him, Adam would have been happier had he never seen them at all.

"I hope they taught him more than this, considering all the money I sent him," he thought, as he gazed at nondescript portraits and colourless landscapes.

For months, Adam tried to persuade his son to learn the craft of picture framing. He explained that it was not only the trade of chisel and wood. It was, rather, the art of understanding a picture. A painting was the soul, while the frame was its body: they could not exist without one another.

"I've known many, many pictures that would fade overnight from an unsuitable frame. And, likewise, frames that would fall off pictures, in protest, no matter how strong the glue was. Pictures and frames have a life of their own, and breathe together. Thus, to offer the wrong frame to a picture is the same as walking in shoes two sizes smaller than your feet."

For months, Sebastian ignored his father's suggestion, claiming that he was either too exhausted or not in the right mood. Finally, after Adam stopped paying the bills for his nightly tippling, Sebastian agreed that he would learn framing, though only after his exhibition. He also extorted a promise from Adam to make the frames for the twenty paintings which would go on display. Adam was angry, but eventually agreed, comforting himself with the thought that parental love had no logical limits anyway.

That year, Adam's advice and skill in framing were so highly valued in Toronto that painters vied to have his frames on their work. His workshop filled with paintings and the Gallery's till with money. Mr. Grieg was so happy that he found himself incapable of denying Adam's request to have his son's exhibition at the gallery, going so far as to promise the main floor.

Adam worked on the promised frames every night. In the month before the exhibition only the sounds of his chisel, wooden hammer, and strange coaxing language could be heard from his tiny room. I do not know how much truth there is in the story that he talked to the wood or that he could speak the language of forests, but it is true that he never used a single nail when joining parts of the frame. He used only glue, out of a wish not to offend the wood.

Mr. Grieg was bothered that Adam devoted so much of his attention to his son's exhibition, ignoring his regular work. He watched the master grow increasingly thin and more taciturn. But on the night before Sebastian's exhibition, when the paintings were mounted in their frames and put up on the walls, Mr. Grieg was overwhelmed by the beauty of what he saw. Whatever the paintings lacked, the elaborately carved frames provided. If a portrait was nondescript, its thick frame portrayed over a dozen of the same carved faces in different moods. If the painting of a foaming sea lacked force, the frame was made up of waves so skilfully sculpted that it seemed as though they would crash through at any moment. A flock of seagulls was sculpted so powerfully that only the fact that they were made of wood prevented them from soaring.

Next morning, Jovan swore to the police that he had spent the whole night in the Gallery. No, he told them, he had not fallen asleep. Nor had he seen any thieves. The door had not been forced. The detectives scratched their heads, uncertain of what to make of Sebastian's paintings, scattered across the floor. Only the frames had disappeared. There were no signs of forced entry. It was as if they had taken off by themselves.

The same day, Sebastian dumped his paintings in the garbage, picked up his things, and left. Two days later, Adam also said good-bye to Mr. Grieg. On that day, the Art Gallery of Ontario was closed to visitors, who were exasperated to hear the odd explanation that the paintings were not ready for viewing. The paintings in the Gallery were mourning.

"You do not need me here any longer," Adam said and left.

He departed with only his bag of tools, so thin that he resembled a frame in search of its painting.

ACKNOWLEDGEMENTS

The stories "Nina," "Minefield" and "Another Bear" were originally translated by Slobodan Drakulic and Patricia Albanese; "The Story of Sinan," "Saturday," and "The Legend of Adam The Frame" by Milica Babic; "A Story about Soil" by Amela Simić and "The Game" by Visnja Brcic. The stories as they appear in this collection are quite different from other appearances and manifestations because, over such a long period of writing (1994-2004), it proved impossible to resist the temptation to rework some of the characters and dramas. Other changes were suggested by friends who read the manuscript, or through the give and take of the editorial process.

Some of these stories have been previously published in *Descant*, *Canadian Forum*, *NWT* (Belgia) and included in the books *Coming Attractions 01* (Oberon Press) and *Making Meaning* (Art Gallery of Ontario). "Minefield" has been made into a short film by Vitold Vidic (Toronto). Other stories have been adapted into radio plays and broadcasted on the National Radio of Bosnia-Herzegovina in 2004.

The author owes special gratitude to Maggie Helwig, Fraser Sutherland and Ann Ireland, as well as to my editor and publisher Daniel Wells.

Special gratitude also goes out to the Canada Council for the Arts.

Yesterday's People is dedicated to my daughter Luna, and to my son Darije.

Typeset in Adobe Garamond by Dennis Priebe,
Yesterday's People was printed offset on Rolland Zephyr Antique Laid
and Smyth-sewn at Gaspereau Press in an edition of 750 copies.
The jacket was printed letterpress from photopolymer plates.
An additional 25 copies were case-bound
by Daniel Wells.

BIBLIOASIS
WINDSOR, ONTARIO